ENTER THE BODY

ALSO BY
JOY McCULLOUGH

YOUNG ADULT

Blood Water Paint

We Are the Ashes, We Are the Fire

Great or Nothing

ENTER THE BODY

JOY McCULLOUGH

DUTTON BOOKS

DUTTON BOOKS
An imprint of Penguin Random House LLC, New York

First published in the United States of America by Dutton Books,
an imprint of Penguin Random House LLC, 2023
First paperback edition published 2024

Visit us online at PenguinRandomHouse.com.

THE LIBRARY OF CONGRESS HAS CATALOGED THE HARDCOVER EDITION AS FOLLOWS:

Names: McCullough, Joy, author. | Title: Enter the body / Joy McCullough. | Description:
New York: Dutton Books, 2023. | Audience: Ages 14 and up. | Audience: Grades 10–12. |
Summary: In the room beneath a theater stage, the ghosts of Juliet, Ophelia, Cordelia, and
other teenage girls who died tragically in Shakespeare's plays, share their experiences and
trauma and get the chance to retell the stories of their lives in their own terms. | Identifiers:
LCCN 2022050509 (print) | LCCN 2022050510 (ebook) | ISBN 9780593406755
(hardback) | ISBN 9780593406762 (ebook) | Subjects: CYAC: Novels in verse. |
Shakespeare, William, 1564-1616. Romeo and Juliet—Fiction. | Shakespeare, William,
1564-1616. Hamlet—Fiction. | Shakespeare, William, 1564-1616. King Lear—Fiction. |
Characters in literature—Fiction. | Teenage girls—Fiction. | Theater—Fiction. | LCGFT:
Novels in verse. | Psychological fiction. | Drama. | Classification: LCC PZ7.5.M435 En
2023 (print) | LCC PZ7.5.M435 (ebook) | DDC 822.3/3—dc23/eng/20230125
LC record available at https://lccn.loc.gov/2022050509
LC ebook record available at https://lccn.loc.gov/2022050510

ISBN 9780593406779
1st Printing

Printed in the United States of America

LSCH
Design by Anna Booth
Text set in Alegreya regular and Adobe Caslon Pro

For anyone who's ever wanted to retell their story

DRAMATIS PERSONAE
(IN ORDER OF THEIR APPEARANCE IN WILLIAM SHAKESPEARE'S PLAYS)

PRINCIPAL PLAYERS

LAVINIA	Daughter of King Titus Andronicus; nineteen; enigmatic (and bloody)
JULIET	Daughter of Lord Capulet of Verona; thirteen; eager (despite the knife in her chest)
OPHELIA	Daughter of Polonius, advisor to the king of Denmark; fifteen; ethereal (and drenched)
CORDELIA	Daughter of King Lear; seventeen; driven (with bruising around her neck)

SUPPORTING PLAYERS

JOAN OF ARC	(burned at the stake)
GERTRUDE	(poisoned)
DESDEMONA	(strangled)
EMILIA	(stabbed)
GONERIL	(died by suicide)
REGAN	(poisoned)
LADY MACBETH	(died by suicide)
CLEOPATRA	(bitten by an asp, suicide)

PART ONE

Women may fall,
when there's no strength in men.

—William Shakespeare
Romeo and Juliet, 1597

[TRAP ROOM]

(The trap room beneath all the stages, anywhere. The ghost light is perpetually on, but it illuminates very little. Which makes it easier to keep to oneself.

That woman with blood on her hands, for example, always wanders into the same corner, every time she crashes through that great stage of fools to this space beneath. Muttering to herself, but never to anyone else.

The one in the nightgown with strangle marks around her neck—clutching a handkerchief like it'll save her from these men, these men—she usually heads to a corner too, after the fall. But only because she doesn't know what else to do.

It's a room, but there are infinite corners.

Enough for everyone to avoid the zealot in singed armor who reeks of the fire that burned her. Or the wild-eyed queen who looks as though she died a dozen deaths before she drank the poison that brought her here. The sisters who killed one another definitely need their own corners.

They crash through, again and again, these women, while the boards above their heads creak with the trodding of the ones who live, or die in glory.

It gets to be monotonous.

But now comes a girl the others aren't accustomed to. It's not that she hasn't been down here before. In fact, she arrived before the rest of them, a violent splotch of ink from the quill of the Bard so young he hadn't yet mastered his instrument. She is the first draft to his later masterpieces; without her they don't exist. And yet they can be forgiven for not remembering her; the moment they see her, they do their level bests to shove her from their minds.

You would too. Only I won't let you.

The jolt this first-draft girl receives when her body crumples to the ground is the least of her concerns. Those concerns are pretty evenly tied between the blood that gushes from her mouth, and also from the end of each arm, where hands should be. But hands are not.

She doesn't even bother uncrumpling. What would be the point?

But there's one woman under this stage compelled to help her, one who has known violence herself and is young enough to remember, while old enough to imagine herself maternal, even if she never survives to bear a child. This maternal one—in a flimsy nightgown that is by design transparent when stage lights hit it exactly right—approaches the bloody heap.

She strokes the girl's hair, soothes the frightened creature until she looks up. The woman startles; for a moment she's not certain whether this girl is prey or predator. Perhaps she is covered in someone else's blood?

She is—but not at her choosing. And her lack of hands offers irrefutable evidence that the girl herself has been on the receiving end of some significant evil.

The woman brings forth her handkerchief, the one that causes her such endless trouble on the stage above; she might as well put it to productive use while she has the chance.

It's a ridiculous thing, flimsy as her nightdress and no match for the ghastly amounts of blood streaming down the girl's face. But wielded by one who wishes to be of use, it somehow does what it is meant to do.

The girl is still wrecked; that cannot be undone. But she is no longer a horror show. And after everything she's been through, the miracle is not that she lives, but that she does not want to be alone. She still craves company. She resists the corners.

This girl, her name is Lavinia. Names are important, even if no one says them. Let's say she's nineteen. She considers her options. The woman with the handkerchief has already retreated. The women in the corners are there for a reason.

There are other girls who want nothing to do with corners, though. Cordelia, seventeen, sits in the center of it all. Bedraggled, she's clearly been through some shit, but it's more important than anything that she keep it together, that you not see the struggle.

And nearby, another girl. Ophelia, fifteen, is soaking wet. Absolutely drenched. There may be a few leaves in her hair.

Lavinia watches these girls—calligraphy to her splotch of ink—who resist the corners. They see her, but their gazes glance off her. They are shoving her from their minds, like I said they would. In fairness, they both have a lot going on, even if they aren't missing appendages.

Ophelia is not okay, but she's not trying to conceal it. She is soaking wet, after all. It's pretty hard to hide that something has gone awry. She doesn't just walk around like this, normally, with pond scum clinging to her dress. This is not usual, except for every time the water drags her down and she crashes into this purgatory.

Cordelia is used to ignoring Ophelia. But now this third girl is here. Watching. Disturbing the norms of the trap room. Cordelia thought she was alone. She's used to being alone. Her own sisters are there, each in their own corners, and even they don't glance toward her. It's not that Cordelia likes it this way; it's just the only way it's ever been, even up above, and how on earth is she supposed to adjust to something new at this point?

Anyway.

Here they are. For a while. Time doesn't mean much in this place. They've just arrived, or maybe they've languished for an eternity, when Juliet crashes through.

Juliet, age thirteen, is also not okay. This is evidenced by the dagger in her heart. She's making a big production of it too. Even Cordelia can't look away as the girl wrenches the dagger from her chest and makes a show of figuring out where to put it. Like it matters.

Ophelia considers approaching her, helping her. She's not sure how, or if she's allowed, as though there are rules here. But when your world has been com-posed entirely of rules—rules that landed you here, in fact—it's a difficult adjustment.

Lavinia flinches at the sight of the dagger. She's safe now—at least until she's called back up and it starts all over again—but logic is nothing against her memories of what a blade can do. Anyway, it's not like she could help; she doesn't have hands.

Cordelia works hard to act as though the others aren't there. She has had enough of dramatic, bleeding girls to last a lifetime. Or an eternity, as it were.

Once Juliet figures out the dagger situation—all she has to do is release it and it's gone, which is a lesson that might have been valuable to learn sooner, but what this eternity has no time for is regret—her gaze lands on Lavinia.

And then darts away—I told you it would—and searches desperately for something else, someone else to latch on to. It's harder for Juliet to shove La-vinia from her mind. Perhaps it's their shared experience with daggers. Per-haps it's her youth. She would have nightmares, if sleep were permitted here.

Ophelia allows her eye to be caught. She understands Juliet's panic and glances apologetically toward Cordelia, as though it's her fault this other girl won't acknowledge their presence.

Juliet isn't bothered. It won't be the first time she's been required to wrest at-tention from the unwilling.)

A ROSE BY ANY OTHER NAME

You think me weak
that I would plunge
a blade into my heart
because the boy I loved
lay lifeless at my side.

But love is weakness.
Love is ripping out
your beating heart, laid bare
to the slings and arrows
of outrageous fortune.

Or maybe that vulnerability
is a kind of strength.
Hard to say
while the blood
drains from my body.

Here's what I knew of love
growing up in that house:

My nursemaid's devotion
above all else.

Father's love of his name,
his wealth, himself.

Servants rutting
behind the stables,
perhaps not love
but want at least.

And Mother?
Mother found
less love than I
in the House of Capulet.

Mother was a child
when betrothed to my father.
You think that's the way of things,
but that's a lie, a symmetrical heart.

      (A lie unearthed
      when Father wished
      to ally himself
      with the House of Paris.)

The other girls Mother's age
waded in the creek
and braided the hair
of dolls they loved more
than Father would ever love

as Mother was led
to the marriage bed,
a seed planted
that could never bear fruit.

So many seeds sown
but if planted
in unprepared soil
they won't have
what they need
        to grow.

Any decent farmer
knows that.

Finally my seed took root
when Mother was no longer a child,
a miracle considering
the wreckage of her body
after so many unborn children.

Some gone
before she knew they grew.
Some just as her belly began to round,
would tear off pieces of her heart
as they fled her body.

And some survived
until she summoned
all her strength
to push them through
a passage not meant to be breached
an ocean through a pinprick
and out they'd come
skin blue and cold.

By the time I arrived
pink and needy
she could barely look upon me.

She looked upon the altar instead
the church offering not love
but certainty and structure.

It started before I was born.
When she could not control
her womb, she could memorize her scripture,
make her confessions, complete her penance.

And then I arrived, but
I too was unpredictable.
She dragged me to Mass
where I watched the weight
roll off her shoulders
as I squirmed on the hard pews
through endless liturgies
that could never surprise
or disappoint her.

Poor little rich girl
the servants might say
if they heard my woes.
I never wanted for anything
                              but love.

A fortune's worth
of dolls and ribbons,
feasts and balls,
gowns and trinkets.

Who was I to complain
if Mother was cold
and Father was
                    Father?

Even Nurse
who truly showered me
with adoration,
listened to my every woe
and wove her love
into every mended seam,
careful curl, bawdy joke.

Even she loved me
like a daughter.

Like
     a daughter.

A substitute
for Susan,
the one she lost.
Most of the time
that was enough.

I always knew
my course was set.
The perfect daughter
until I became
the perfect wife.

Still, I used to daydream
of a life like Susan's.

      (If my beloved nurse's
      child had lived.)

Simple cot
in servants' quarters,
garments the same,
day unto day.
Fingers raw from
scrubbing dishes or
soiled laundry or
hauling water for
the mistress's bath

but also
a kind of freedom
in clear roles
in honest work

and the chance
to marry for love.

[TRAP ROOM]

(In the trap room, one woman shifts from her corner, agitated. She's tempted to interrupt, tell this girl who wanted for nothing how ungrateful she was, how foolish to throw it all away. To stab a sword through her own heart.

As far as this woman is concerned, clear roles and honest work can just as easily get you run through by the sword of the one you married for love.

But no one notices this woman's agitation. Just like they didn't notice her up above.

Ophelia listens, rapt, to Juliet's story. Verona is far from Denmark, but Ophelia feels at home in the tale of complicated families.

Cordelia relates more than she'd like, to feeling like a pawn in someone else's game.

And Lavinia? No hands, no tongue, but her ears work perfectly, and Lavinia is listening still.)

Before Romeo
I met Count Paris at the ball
and knew why he was there.

Handsome, wealthy,
smooth as his kidskin gloves
but subtle as Nurse
at the bottom of a bottle.

Subtle or not
he would wait.
Father wouldn't marry
me off so soon.

But Father introduced us,
        cheeks already ruddy
        from dance and drink
but not so far gone
he couldn't envision our family
allied to a count.
Father pushed me into
the arms of that titled man,
who chuckled at me
as though I'd thrown myself.

As we danced
Count Paris
gripped my waist
too tight

breathed hot
on my face

and trod
on my toes.

But he spoke
kindly, painted
lovely pictures
of his estate
his horses
his gardens.

Asked
my favorite
flower.

He did not repel me
and I thought

      it could be worse.

The moment I locked eyes
across a crowded
sea of dancers
with a boy
whose gaze
burned through me
his name irrelevant

an unfamiliar spark ignited
a flame of white-hot anger:

> Why should I settle
> for *could be worse?*

> Why should I be denied
> desires of my own?

> Why should I perform perfection
> for people who fall so short?

Hunger
like I've never known,
the all-consuming need
to absorb the entirety of this soul
whose every breath syncs up with mine.

Once I'd felt that grip on my gut
that racing pulse
desperate want

how could I ever
be satisfied
with less?

We don't jump, intentional.
Shuffle, unsure.
We don't confidently strut
or crawl in despair.
We're not dropped
by some unseen hand,
we don't squeeze in
or glide with grace.
We don't sprint (even when
some might claim we're rushing).
And we don't soar heavenward.

We fall.

Tumbling head over heels
we don't know which way
is up, can't control our limbs,
smash into innocents along the way,
are bruised and battered and

so alive.

The first time I fell
I was dropped
into a life
I didn't choose.

This time
as I hurtled toward Romeo

I fell away
from that role
I was supposed to play,
a sudden escape

through an unseen trapdoor,
sleight-of-hand stage magic

and I was gone.

Montague

a name meant
to augment an ego
an age ago

a mean moat
man get gone
ante unmet

a mate not man
gent to mount
mute a moan
untame a tongue

one man a gem

Capulet

a petal teacup
cute lace pleat

                  leap

a plea acute

let a pale pact cut a tale

Shedding garments
in my room that night
each brush of fabric
across skin on fire,
my nurse believed
I'd reached the bottom
of my own bottle.

Twirling in my chemise,
clutching gown to chest,
drinking in the scent of the boy
who had pressed up against it,
perhaps I would never stop dancing.

     I'm dizzy just
     looking at you.

I laughed at my nurse,
pressed the gown into her arms,
danced my way out

     to the balcony.

My favorite place
in the entire world
was the balcony
off my chambers.

Father owned all,
Mother ruled the staff,
but this one space
was my dominion.

Even Nurse never
stepped past the door.
Perhaps heights frightened her
but more likely she realized
I needed one space
to be messy and true.

One space
to weep and rage
and sing and dance
and dream and grieve
before I pulled myself back

into the girl I had to be.

I called his name
into the night
because I could

because no one
would hear my cry

and I loved
how it felt
in my mouth

and maybe
a part of me
believed
he would hear,

we were so connected
that no matter
where he was
he'd know I called for him
and he'd call back.

When he did
my heart careened
in mad circles
through my chest
and up my throat
and out into the night.

He was there
when I called.
Of course he was.

But also, saints and angels, how
was he there beneath my window,
this boy, a Montague, who risked his life
to stand on Capulet grounds?

And why was he down on the ground
and not up in my arms, why
didn't the intensity of his love
propel him up through the air
defy the force that kept
him pinned to earth
for we were stronger
than mere laws of nature.

Feuds handed down
through generations,
an heirloom to a toddler
who cannot understand its value
but quickly learns
what happens when
it isn't prized above all else.

Hate learned before letters,
a name more vile
than the coarsest insult

      filthy whoreson
      heir of a mongrel bitch
      plague-sore
      puke-stocking
      lump of foul deformity

but nothing's worse than Montague.

One love couldn't change
the course of things,
a seagull's breath
against the ocean's tides.

Could we even call it love,
this spark ignited when palm met palm
and turned to raging inferno that threatened
to incinerate the world around us?

Whatever it was, it drove Romeo
to my garden, my heart,
drove me to dream beyond
the hate I'd learned.

Perhaps a seagull's breath
could turn the tides.

When I returned
to my room a new girl,
Nurse must have known
my scarlet cheeks didn't burn for Paris.

Of course she knew,
for at the ball I sent her
to learn Romeo's name.
Oh, dear, dear Nurse.

> *How nice for you*
> *to get some air.*

She let down my hair
with a twinkle in her eye.

> *It's done you well,*
> *that glow upon your cheeks.*

A giggle bubbled up.
I waited for her scolding,
her warning against
such foolish dreams.

> *I think you ought to make a habit*
> *of taking the air in the evenings.*
> *For your health, of course.*

I threw my arms around her
for I could not hold Romeo
and I had so much love to give.

My tongue bled
through breakfast
as I bit back
every new word
and touch and feeling
I'd come to know
from one day to the next.

Instead Father regaled us with tales
of the ball we all attended
as though we hadn't been there,
applauded himself for his hosting prowess.
Mother gripped her fork so tight
I thought she might bend metal.

I barely listened until

    Montague.

Why would he speak
the name of my love?
He didn't speak it like I would,
a wish, a kiss, a song.
Did he see when we danced?
When our hearts became one?

But now he spoke
of Tybalt, my cousin,
who, though I'm fond,
had nothing to do with
matters of my heart.

What of Tybalt and the Montagues?

Mother and Father both froze,
forks halfway to their mouths.
Had I ever expressed
the slightest interest
in their pointless feud?

> *Young Tybalt*
> *nearly turned the ball into a brawl*
> *when he spotted a Montague in disguise.*

My heart caught.
Father knew Romeo was there?
And did nothing?
That was very nearly
cause for hope.

> *I don't know why*
> *you stopped him.*

Mother's voice was petulant,
nonsensical. Would she prefer
the ball have turned to bloodshed?

> *He caused no harm.*
> *None but Tybalt*
> *even realized*
> *he was there.*

None but Tybalt

> save myself
> my nurse
> the other girls
> whose heads he turned.

No one realized

> which means of course
> that Father didn't realize,
> and there is no one else
> who matters.

[TRAP ROOM]

(In the trap room, there is a moment, a thrum of recognition.

These girls, these women, they're queens and ladies' maids, spanning centuries, slain by their own hands or by another's, but they've all felt this shifting ground, this realization that their own experiences are of no consequence to a man they've trusted.

Not only of no consequence, but their experiences can be leverage used against them by a man they've trusted. By a father. Lavinia's wounds bleed more freely as her heartbeat accelerates.)

When Nurse delivered
a note from my love
I thrilled to the strokes
from his pen, the way he knew
I ached to see him. He sent word
of a meeting place where no one
cared about our names.

You must take me to Friar Laurence!

Nurse laughed as she made up my bed.

      Look who's the little despot today!
      Love does make one tyrannical.
      Why, my Susan—

Nurse!

I usually allowed her
to prattle on about
her long-lost Susan
but now was not the time
to linger on a mother's love.
I had other things to linger on now.

My sky-blue dress.
Hair up, I think. Or down?

      Taking great pains
      to impress the Holy Father?

I shoved the note into her hands
    (she claimed not to read
    but had puzzled out
    private notes before)
and went to retrieve the dress myself.

The friar's door opened
with a heady rush of scents,
his ceiling an upside-down forest
of herbs bound together.

His eyes twinkled.

> *Signorina Capulet. Would you*
> *to the chapel for confession?*

I suppose
I had much
to confess,
though in truth
I felt
more sinned against
than sinning.

Behind me, Nurse chuckled,
then the friar did too.

> *Do not keep me from her*
> *a moment longer!*

At Romeo's voice
my heart split open.
I rushed past the teasing friar
and there he was,
most beautiful of creatures.
High cheekbones, perfect lips,
eyes I could live in forever.

We'd only just met the night before.
Could my feelings be real?
That was like asking if the wind blows.
The wind is not visible, a grounded thing,
but it's real as a hurricane.

He stepped forward, hand outstretched.

My rose.

I was in his arms
before I could ponder
more foolish questions.

Father wished me
to marry a man
I'd barely met.

Mother wished me
to be good and pure.

What was impure
about the harmony
of two souls singing together?

All thoughts of objections
vanished when his lips met mine.
How could these notes ever be discordant?

When Friar Laurence coughed,
we broke apart, but Romeo kept
my hand in his.

> *Come, Friar,*
> *you believe in love.*

Friar Laurence smiled,
his weathered face betraying his years
enough for countless loves
beyond his bride, the church.

> *I do.*
> *I also believe in peace.*

The friar consented to marry us
believing our union could bring Verona
into harmony of its own.

If we asked permission
our parents would object
if not declare all-out war.

But if we came to them
joined in holy matrimony
by the holy friar
offering holy peace,
how could they profane our union?

These were the friar's reasons.
Romeo and I needed none other
than the spark that traveled
from his hand to mine and back again.

I, Juliet Capulet,
take you, Romeo Montague

for my husband

to have and to hold
from this day forward

for better, for worse
for richer, for poorer

in sickness and health

> till death us depart.

I stumbled through the day
a secret bride,
cradling close
the choice I'd made.

Nobody knew
save Nurse and the friar
and while I couldn't believe
that everyone who saw me
didn't see my transformation,
didn't notice the world off its axis,
I also did not mind keeping our love
a private thing a while longer,
a hidden jewel in my heart.

I could not comprehend
why Nurse came to me
with such anguish upon her face.

What now, dear Nurse?
Nothing can bring me down today!

> *Oh, child. There's been a brawl,*
> *Montagues and Capulets*
> *drawing swords and spilling blood.*

My heart stopped.
The hidden jewel
pierced through.

My Romeo?

> *Not slain. But, child—*

The rest could not matter
if Romeo was safe.
Whatever she said,
whoever was dead,
I'd grieve, but not
as though my life was over
because it lived
in my Montague.

Your cousin Tybalt—

Oh, dear Tybalt!
Tempestuous soul!
My relief at Romeo's fortune
couldn't stop the tears for Tybalt,
though I'd always known
he would leave us far too young.
One could not survive this world
with such a fiery heart.

*—slain by the sword
of your Romeo.*

But that was false.
Romeo would never
have killed my kinsman.
Even before he loved me
his gentle nature kept him away
from the feuding in Verona's streets.

He wouldn't.
You're wrong.

He did not start it
but your cousin killed
his dearest friend, Mercutio.

Panic rose. My love
was peaceable, but loyal.
His comrade dead in the streets,
he might not stop to think
of Tybalt as my kinsman.

Still, Tybalt!
Tybalt who shielded me
through childhood,
more brother than cousin,
always my defender.

A sob ripped from my throat.
Nurse stroked my hair
willed my heart to keep beating.

Oh, child.
There's more.

How could there be more?
Tybalt was dead,
but Romeo alive.
I was not certain
I could look him in the face,
but at least he lived.

Your Romeo
is banished.

Capulet + Montague

a couple
a couplet

a pageant, a glance
put palm to palm

name an omen
an open plea

molten tongue
open petal

plot plan
moan alone

a poet gone
plunge atone

      complete lament

banished
from Verona

banished
from justice

banished
from the chance for peace

the chance
to charm Mother
earn Father's respect

but never
banished
from my heart.

When I saw him again
the grief in his eyes
sliced through me
like the sword
that slew Tybalt.

My rose.

Romeo fell
   (tumbling, smashing)
to the ground, prostrate.

> *I do not ask your forgiveness*
> *for I do not deserve it*
> *but I couldn't leave*
> *without telling you*
> *I will forever grieve your cousin*
> *alongside my dear Mercutio*
> *but most of all I'll grieve*
> *what might have been between us.*

I fell
   (bruised, battered)
to my knees before him.

I do ask your forgiveness
for the brief moments
when I doubted if I could love
the one who killed my Tybalt.
I can and do.

You shouldn't.
The bloodshed—

Is on the hands of every one of us
who lives without protesting,
without asking what it's for.

I didn't strike to kill—

I know.

I'd give my life for his—

I'd rather die.

But I have caused you pain
and banishment is not
sufficient punishment.

Your banishment
is the deepest wound.
To never see you again—

The tears I barely shed
for Tybalt bleeding on the stones
tumbled out, aggrieved,
ashamed, and angry all at once.
The Prince banished Romeo
for killing Tybalt, killed
for slaying Mercutio, killed
for ancient grievances

nobody can recall. We should all
be condemned to death.

    My love.

I fell
    (sleight of hand, I'm gone)
into his arms,
pressed lips upon his own,
no longer able to bear the sound
of words, words, words
solving nothing
only digging us deeper
in this rubble, which will
bury us all.

I pushed him toward the bed;
he stumbled back, surprised.

My lips were frantic, hands
tugging as though I could pull
him so close he'd never leave.

This time he was not
a boy I'd danced with,
boy I'd kissed, but man
I called my husband.

I didn't need
the blessing of the church
to know I needed this boy,
I needed this man beside me.

We fell onto the bed,
a mess of limbs, teeth crashing
sobs and laughter intermingled.

A moment's hesitation—
he was the only boy I'd ever kissed.
But he was old enough, I knew
his lips had touched countless others . . .

He pulled away, trailed
a finger down my face.

Like a doll.

I'm not—

> *Your perfect skin.*

Stop.

His hands stilled,
he scrambled away.

> *I'm sorry.*
> *This was too fast.*
> *We don't have to—*

It's not that.

I grew up
hearing women spoken of
as dolls to play with and discard.

Mother and her church
taught me purity was all I had
to offer. And purity meant
chaste and innocent
while all around me
the streets ran with blood.

By that measure, purity
is gone the moment a man
has discarded the doll.
A whole life striving
for something that's gone
in an instant
for another's pleasure,
                    power.

[TRAP ROOM]

(Time freezes. Such as time is down here.

The main thing is, there's a stylistic break. For this moment, no one in the trap room listens to Juliet's story. They'll be back; she hasn't lost her audience.

For now, they're each considering their wounds:

> *the missing limbs*
> *the blistering burns*
> *the gaping stabs*
> *the grayish pallor of poison*
> *the bite marks of an asp*

Each considers how these acts of violence against their bodies were acceptable to the world, while their desires were not.)

Romeo's doll
is different.
Not a worthless toy.

A treasure that would be loved
even when the cloth has worn thin,
the dress ragged, eyes popped off
and mouth a faint echo
of the ruby lips it started with.

If we could have the life
we chose, away from feuds,
I'd be his doll eternally,
even after decades of love,
as we helped each other down the hall
to reach our bed, tucked in together
against the cold, against the world.

Juliet.
We are wed
whether we seal this
with want or with tears.

I want you.

I know.
But you don't have to
do anything
besides breathe
for me to be content forever.

I would not be content.
I wanted him.
I wanted him with desire
more pure than any abstinence.

I pushed him
onto his back.

I want
everything.

Mother never told me
what goes on in the marital bed,
though she'd spoken
with nothing but disgust
of how her lost babies
had taken root.

The previous day I'd overheard
two servants boast of how they'd thrust
a woman against a wall, no love
in their display of power, brute force.

Nurse had jested all my life
about the physical act—no love
in what she said, but fun.
I hadn't understood.

As I grew to piece it all together
I saw my ignorance was part of her game.
I played along, the innocent poppet,
gathering scraps of knowledge
I'd find nowhere else.

But this, right here, in Romeo's arms:

no one spoke of this.

He was sweet and slow
but something desperate
unfurled inside me.

I needed his skin on mine
I needed his lips everywhere
I needed his hands holding me together
or I might split into a thousand pieces

his skin was hot; I dove into the flame
his lips, his tongue, his hands
traversed lands I'd never explored

I was shattered and whole and his

and mine

When we lay together
in the rumpled sheets,
floating back into our bodies

I examined my hand in his.
I wasn't stained
or used up.

I was the same girl
I'd been before

only now I had
even more to give.

Cruel sunlight
wrenched him away
leaving me bereft,
his absence frosting over my skin.

Nurse would doubtless prod and poke,
merciless in her teasing, but I was ready.
Eager even to speak to the only one
who could understand.

But she came in strange, distant.

Oh, Nurse!

I sat up, dragging blanket
round my shoulders
to ward against the chill.

Why did you never tell me—

    Hush, child.

She set a simple gown
upon my bed, dreary brown,
fit for a convent.

*Not this! Rose, I think.
Or violet? No, rose—*

    *Your father comes
    to speak with you;
    get up quickly, dress.*

To speak with me?
This morning?

Had Father learned of my marriage?

    For mercy's sake, get dressed!
    You'll be the death of me, my girl.

Not only Father, Mother too.
I'd barely fastened up my bodice
when in they came
as though we gathered
in my chambers every morning.

I'd worn the brown
for Nurse had never been so serious
and now I feared another death.

(And still I could not stop the heat
from rising in my cheeks, the rumpled sheets
reminding me that what I wanted mattered.)

    You look well, daughter.

        She always does.
        Our beautiful girl.

Mother's voice was sincere
but her gaze shrewd.
Could she see, did she know?

      Yes, yes. She'll make
      a lovely bride.

He did know!
Or wait, *she'll make . . .*
He said it as a thing
still to come.

The time is here.
You are to marry
Count Paris,
darling girl.

My eyes flew to Nurse,
grim in the corner.
This was not about Romeo,
not about peace or love.

Isn't this exciting?
A dress of lace,
pearls in your hair—

Mother was a twisted reflection
of my glee the night of the ball
when I first met my love.

We'll plan the grandest feast
for all Verona!

No time for that.
A simple affair,
on Thursday, I think.

Thursday?!

Bile rose in my throat

      I had no regrets

blood roared in my ears

      I had to tell them

I gasped for air

      I could not be wed
      when my heart was another's
      and my body was mine

I grasped for words.

So soon, Father?
Tybalt is barely
cold in his crypt—

Mother gasped and I regretted
my thoughtless words
but she would regret more
if I were forced into mortal sin.

And even if proper mourning
was not the root of my objection,
I was right. There was no need to rush.

> *Exactly why we need this.*
> *A distraction, cause for celebration*
> *rather than a war. At least*
> *the wretched Montague*
> *who killed him will never*
> *walk these streets again.*

This time I was the one to gasp,
followed by a sob I could not contain.

> *Come now, child.*
> *Your cousin*
> *would welcome*
> *your happy marriage.*

I can't.
I won't.
I'm sorry.

The first time Father
brought up Count Paris
as a marriage prospect,
I demurred.

I had not yet met Romeo.
I never expected to marry for love
but I couldn't fathom marriage
at my age, to a man I barely knew.

Father was patient.
There was time, he told Paris.

Now, though,
perhaps because
I'd contradicted him again

and rather than hesitate
I'd outright told him no

Father no longer
saw fit to indulge
my right to an opinion.

You, my child, are unworthy
yet I have arranged his match for you.

You'll go to the church to be wed
or I will drag you there by your hair.

"I can't"
"I won't"
"I'm sorry"

I'm sorry you're
a disobedient wretch.
Speak not. Reply not.
Do not answer me.

[TRAP ROOM]

(Juliet falters. She's young, caught up in telling a tale of tragedy, yes, but also romance, and then along comes this moment, which was awful enough when it unfolded but made worse in retrospect.

The others feel it. Especially Lavinia, who knows of enraged fathers and who longs to be of comfort. But how?

It's not the end of Juliet's tale. For one thing, the dagger hasn't appeared yet. Everyone knows you can't introduce a dagger in the beginning of a story without plunging it into something by the end. But Juliet is done telling it. At least for now.

That's fair. When one's father has threatened to drag one by the hair into a forced marriage, a few moments of pause are reasonable.

Cordelia is not unmoved by Juliet's story. She is not, after all, made of stone. And she knows a thing or two about fathers who place their needs above their daughters'. But still she keeps to herself.

There is silence for a time. There it is again, time. Both weighing down and stretching out. Juliet is tempted to press on, for the telling of stories holds back the weight of time.

Ophelia decides to fill the silence. If nothing else to give the younger girl a break, for she is clearly not ready to continue.

So Ophelia will speak. She had so few chances before.)

PRAY YOU, LOVE, REMEMBER

1.

There was a time
I lived
not
as a
stone
wedged into
unyielding walls

but a
leaf on
a branch
on a tree in a garden
moved by wind and rain
and scuttling bugs.

But leaves
fall.

2.

The stones didn't always choke.
The court was grand at first
imposing, enchanting,
a fairy tale and I

      the girl at the center.

At least that's what I thought.
And wouldn't you?

a castle
a garden
a prince

with eyes
you could drown in

3.

The royal grounds
burst with blooms, treetops
striving toward the sun, birds
singing a chorus of joy and want
like the women Mother once gathered
beneath her wing.

Here we would be safe from plague,
Father advising the king,
while my brother, Laertes,
learned from the brilliant men
surrounding us.

And I?
I would seek new shelter
in the absence of my mother's wing.

4.

With endless days stretched out before me,
a barren field replacing the jumbled garden
of friends and neighbors I'd left behind,
no one should have been surprised
when one bright wildflower caught my eye.

Perhaps the surprise
was that I caught the prince's eye as well.

A perfect fairy tale, don't you think?
Mercurial prince, fated to marry
for power and alliance, duty

       and the advisor's daughter,
             who loved him with her wild, aching heart.

It's only a fairy tale
if the prince loves her back.

5.

Maybe the real fairy tale unfolded
before we ever reached the court,
a family in a comfortable cottage
with ivy twining up the walls,
fragrant rosemary lining the walk
to a front door nearly always open

to souls who needed tea, sympathy,
a piece of my mother's heart,
which only seemed to grow
the more it was pruned back,
a wild, untamed thing, a blackberry bramble
with only sweet fruit and nary a thorn.

A brother who played his part to perfection,
pulling my hair and stealing my sweets,
then shielding me from harm and weaving
flower wreaths he set upon my curls.
I always knew he'd grow, but didn't understand
that he would grow beyond my reach

an oak towering over my dandelion,
to a time beyond flower wreaths
where he could no longer fathom
a circlet upon my head or that
another boy might crown me.

A father of ideas, words, and quill,
always thinking, feet firmly fixed

upon the ground, deep roots.
But his mind was always moving, leaves
in the wind until he wound his branches
all the way to a spot beside the king.

Once upon a time
he cared

what I thought and dreamed.

6.

We remained at the cottage
while Father journeyed
back and forth to the castle.

Mother insisted we stay
because if her doors
were not open
who would welcome
the strays? Who would
make them tea, and listen?

Perhaps there were strays
in the castle, Father said.
Mother laughed.

But Father
was always
wise.

7.

Then came the chills.

An invasive vine
squeezing her head,
forcing out all reason.

Mother withered
like lobelia in full sun,
unable to welcome visitors at all.

The tender, swollen lumps
on her pale, beautiful neck
sent Father racing for a doctor.

But for all the people
Mother had stitched together,
she could not be saved.

Pray you, love, remember.

[TRAP ROOM]

(In the trap room, the women remember.

They remember mothers lost to plagues, to violence, to childbirth. They remember mothers so immaterial they never even trod the stage. Cordelia's mother, only invoked as an insult. Ophelia's and Lavinia's mothers never mentioned at all.

These maternal stories are so insignificant the audience must imagine characters sprung fully formed from their fathers' heads. The audience doesn't struggle with this; they've done it time and time again.

But the Bard didn't write a play about Athena. Every single one of these women had a mother, whether or not we ever knew her story.)

8.

Sometimes I wonder
why I didn't fight
my father, brother,
fight to stay
in the only home
I'd ever known,
the one with Mother's
tendrils hooked into every crevice.

The home made of stones
soaked with tears
from every soul
who ever had a joy
or sorrow to share.

Sometimes I wonder
if the long purples
I planted the first day
Mother was too weak
to embrace a visitor
have grown so tall
they've buried the house
like Mother's body
in the churchyard,
too good for this world.

9.

At the time
it made sense
to leave the cottage,
transplant our broken family
away from the endless sympathies,
mourners who needed more
than we had to give.

Even if it hadn't
I wouldn't have objected.
Father didn't shed a tear
when Mother died, but the slightest nudge
might be the thing to unleash a torrent
to drown us all.

The cold stone walls
were perfect mirrors
for what we all felt.

We were
no longer meant
for a cozy cottage
filled with love.

10.

At first I couldn't
meet his eyes.
Across a table piled high with food
he sat, the only other person
younger than the stones around us.

He tried to speak to me.
I wanted to answer
but a flower wilts
when the sun burns
bright upon it.

Later, in the great room
where Queen Gertrude's joyful laugh
rang out above the posturing talk of men,
I perched on the edge of it all
longing to escape to the gardens
but knowing my place.

So dull, don't you think?

I startled so intensely
the prince himself jumped back,
recovered, then placed his hand
upon my arm to reassure.
It didn't.

I forgot my place
and fled.

11.

Sometimes I thought
that when Mother died
I expired as well and left behind
a ghost, a shell, invisible girl.

Invisible, no one cared
how I passed my days,
what I thought or felt.
Perhaps my throat had closed,
my voice unused for so long.

To be noticed and seen,
spoken to and touched,
my soul slammed back into my self
and I ran in terror of my own flesh and blood.

12.

The next day he found me
up in my tree.

In several months
of court life, I'd never seen
another human soul
inside these gardens
and the higher I climbed
the closer I was to Mother.

I looked down at the sound
of a plink in the stream.

> *Ah, good,*
> *I was afraid*
> *to startle you.*

The sight of him
had startled me
but not enough
I'd topple
from my branch.

Forgive me, Your Highness.
I'll climb down.

> *Nonsense.*
> *May I climb up?*

I wondered that a prince
would climb a tree
but at my nod
he scrambled up
to a branch opposite mine.

I'm Polonius's daughter.

I don't know why I felt the need
to define myself that way
except to say I belonged there
(though I didn't).

He nodded.

     Ophelia. Helper.

I'm sorry?

     Your name.
     From the Greek for "helper."
     Didn't you know?

I didn't.

[TRAP ROOM]

(A sigh reverberates throughout the trap room, bouncing off the corners, the edges of these women's memories.

Didn't you know?

Sometimes they didn't know, not having been offered the same education as the man who asked the question, or didn't even ask it but pinned them with a withering glare for daring to exist in the world without knowledge they'd been barred from.

More often they did know, but still were pinned to the walls of their stations by men and boys who assumed they couldn't possibly know and proceeded to tell them, under the guise of edification but really so the men could feel superior.

Ophelia is one of the few who didn't feel it like that. She might have, were she inclined to think on her brother, her father.

She'd rather dwell on the thought that she might be a helper to a prince.)

13.

He found me in the tree
most days between his studies
and the evening meal.

I'd ask what he had learned
and he would scoff, dismiss it all as dull,
and ask me to tell him a story.

So I did. Because if a prince
desires something, I serve at the pleasure.
Also, I love stories

and the way his eyes would dance
as the story built, the hero drawing
closer and closer to the edge.

He laughed and gasped and interrupted.
He danced the branch like a balance beam
until I bade him stop.

Sometimes I'd catch myself in joy,
flush full of shame that I should be so happy
in a world without my mother.

14.

I only told a sad tale once.
He let me tell it
but did not dance
or interrupt.

I didn't realize in the telling
how far away he'd gone,
his body in my very tree
but his eyes, his mind
departed.

The story finished,
he grabbed my hand.
It wasn't the first time
but it was different,
desperate.

> *No more sad stories,*
> *I think, my helper.*

Then he leapt to the ground,
          saluted, and was gone.

15.

Gone
to Germany
before I could
tell him the tale
of how my heart leapt
at the sound of his laugh,
how his hunger for my words
filled me up.

It wasn't his choice.
A prince must be
properly educated
and castle tutors would not do.
Off to learn to be a king.

The cold stone walls
became a tomb but every now and then
a letter arrived, his words tumbling across
the page like his laugh, commanding
my attention so fully the world
around me faded.

16.

To the celestial
most beautified Ophelia—

Doubt thou
the stars are fire,
doubt that the sun
doth move,
doubt truth
to be a liar,
but never doubt
                    I love.

Thine evermore,

    Hamlet

17.

I read his letters
again and again
until my hands
smudged the ink
into oblivion
and then
I planted them
beneath our story tree
and daisies grew.

18.

When Hamlet's father died
I did not think as a patriot,
for the country,
but hoped Hamlet
would soon return to court

followed by fear that Father
would no longer have a place
when the prince returned
and I would not be here
to show him the daisies
sprouted from his words.

But the king's brother
ascended the throne,
taking pains not to disrupt
the court any more than
was inevitable upon
a king's death.

Father's place
was secure, and I
in the great hall
with the rest of the court
to welcome Prince Hamlet home.

19.

He did not meet my eye,
not once, as I stood beside
Father, offering our condolences.

But he couldn't, for if he did
he'd find refuge for his tears
and those could not be released
in this place, this company.

He would find me later
at our tree. He would.

Except he didn't.
When I finally
climbed down
from the moonlit branches
I saw our daisies had died.

20.

A week went by,
unending, choking ivy,
until then one day he found me
as I gathered lavender.

   My helper, my love.

That's all he said
before he launched
his weight into my arms,
his sobs coursing through
our bodies made one.

I'm here.

21.

Frantic, clumsy
we stumbled
into his chambers,
the door thudding shut,
just our heartbeats
between these walls.

Don't leave me.

I won't.

His eyes wild,
his hands everywhere
grasping to hold me there
as if I'd ever leave him.

Promise.

With my life.

His lips on my neck
hurried, his fingers fumbling.

I need you.

I'm here.

[TRAP ROOM]

(Cordelia shifts, uncomfortable; she doesn't want to hear this part. She blocked it out when Juliet prattled on about hands and lips, but Ophelia is not some lovesick child. She's a girl being used by a boy who doesn't love her. At least, that's how Cordelia sees it.

Lavinia agrees. But in her role as silent observer, she notices some things Cordelia may miss:

How Juliet sits forward, eager for more details.

How the women in their corners breathe as one, but only inhale. They've been in Ophelia's place, most of them. They want something more for her, something better. But they won't intrude. Their cynicism is not needed here.)

22.

He needed me
like seeds need water.

Water had always seemed
a delicate thing,
a teardrop, a sprinkle of rain.

But water could also
cleave mountains in two,
sustain all life.

I could be water.

23.

Mother never shooed me from the room
when women's talk turned
down an unfamiliar path.
I followed at a distance,
finding the way more familiar
than I'd thought, lined as it was
with Mother's love.

Women wept or laughed or raged
and Mother listened, impressed on them
the wisdom of their bodies,
the validity of their desire,
their pleasure.

When she found my brother
behind the chicken coop
with his hands up the skirt
of a village girl, she sat him down
and spoke of how to treat a partner,
how to listen and fulfill her needs,
till his face was redder
than the rooster's coxcomb.

I don't know
if he heard her

but I did.

24.

My needs mattered too.
And I needed him.

I needed his hands
on my skin, his anchor
to earth, his reminder
that I was substantial,
could be held,
could be filled.

It wasn't only need.
It was want.
He lit me on fire.

25.

He changed like the tide,
one day there and then not.

How he could
light me on fire, then
leave me to burn.

How he could
pen words
of such tenderness

then look through me
as though I were
insubstantial,
a skeletal leaf.

I did not understand.
I'd lost my mother;
I could have shared his grief.

His melancholy wrenched open my own,
brought Mother back to haunt me
with the words she would have said
but couldn't now. The teas she would have made,
balms applied to mend his broken heart.

But I
        I had only stories.

26.

Laertes scoffed
at Hamlet's grief
as though we hadn't also
lost a parent, as though my brother
hadn't also played maids false
since Mother died and left him
to his own impulses.

Father noticed my distress;
I thought he'd comfort me.
Instead he chided me
for thoughts
of love.

A prince
could never
marry me
and even
            if he could . . .

Neither knew what I had seen
in Hamlet's eyes,
how he had danced upon a branch
and let me spin him star-crossed tales
of life beyond the crown.

27.

When Father asked me
to ensnare Hamlet
in conversation
so he and the king
could listen in

I thought
I was helping.

Not them, but Hamlet.
If they could understand
how pure his grief,
they'd come to know him.

Father shoved a prayer book in my hands
upon Hamlet's approach and sent me
to sit in quiet contemplation
in the vestibule.
I longed to tell them
(but wouldn't) that if they wanted
an honest glimpse into Hamlet's state of mind
I should climb a tree and braid a chain of flowers.

Instead I played
the pious girl.

28.

My lord.

> *The beautiful Ophelia.*

Your helper.

> *. . .*

Your helper.
My name?
You used to—

> *I've no idea*
> *what you mean.*

The letters you sent
while you were gone
restored my soul.

> *I sent no letters.*

But, my lord,
you did.
You spoke
of love—

> *I did love you once.*

You did!

I think you might
love me still
but grief clouds
over any rays of light.

          I loved you not.

You just said—

          Where is he?
          Your father?

I'm not sure.
With the king, perhaps?

          Is he here too?

I don't know
what you mean . . .

          They're here.
          They listen in.
          I'm not a fool.

I never said—

          But you are.
          A fool to let them use you.
          A fool to think I'd love you.
          A silly painted girl
          who'll end her days
          as nun or whore,
          it hardly matters.

29.

the stars are fire

the sun doth move

truth is a liar

        he cannot love

30.

We gather that night
to watch traveling players
enact a tragedy, as if
we couldn't simply observe
the souls that wander these halls.

If I could have, I would have
slipped on a mask of my own.
Instead I was displayed
for all to see.
All who'd heard
how I'd been used
and humiliated
by these men,
these men.

There he was,
a knife to my gut
to watch him laughing,
instructing the players
as though he hadn't left me
bleeding on the stones
just hours before.

Despite that,
when it was time
to find our places,
he spurned his mother
and sat with me instead.

31.

It's a nicer view
at your side.

Yes, from here
the players—

Not the players.
You're prettier
than my mother.

Oh.

Prettier still when you blush.

I said nothing.
Silent, I couldn't
be wrong.

Shall I lie in your lap?

What? No!

My head on your lap, I mean.
An innocent thing, you dirty girl.
Though I wouldn't mind
my face between your legs.

We were as much a show
as the frolicking players

though I'd been dragged
unwillingly upon the stage.

He did not mind his volume,
wanted all to hear his crude
and knowing jokes, to see
his mask of bawdy devil-may-care

when underneath
his face was not hard angles
but still the soft boy who did not know
where to put his hands, who cried
when I gave him sanctuary.

32.

Each quip
a separate thrust
of the knife

the wounds ripped further open,
jagged bloody tears
each time I laughed
pretended
my screams
weren't choking me.

Pretended I wasn't begging
time itself to stop,
back up, hurtle forward,
whatever would release me
from this moment.

[TRAP ROOM]

(Lavinia draws another step closer to Ophelia as she tells her tale. The blood no longer gushes from her mouth, her arms. It's more like the occasional drip, which falls and falls and never hits the ground. There may not be a ground.

Lavinia has been in Ophelia's place before, frozen by the razor-edged laughter of boys who'll say what they want about her body, and worse. Part of her wants to find her own corner, like most of the women here. Turn away and try to forget, even though she knows it's impossible. There's some comfort in the attempt, until there's not. But some part of her cannot help drawing nearer to the girls who are bold enough to tell their stories.

The wild-eyed queen has turned from her corner. Not stepped away, mind you. She keeps the solid walls at her back. At least she tells herself they're solid. She listens with special care to Ophelia's tale. Her heart breaks all over again for what she did not do. Regret is the minotaur down here.

And the regret of the mothers, it's the most terrifying monster of all.)

33.

Mother down below the ground
food for flowers, worms, the herbs
you magicked into healing potions,
is there room there where you are?

I could feed the flowers too,
the herbs I'd grow would have more use
in this strange place
than what I have to offer
in this flesh.

34.

I told my tree a story
of a girl who still had friends around the corner,
welcoming arms who gathered her
when she was mistreated by a boy,
dried her tears and made her laugh
with stories of their own
and then they dreamed together
of happier days when they'd find
true love, build families,
and keep them safe within
the walls of their hearts.

I'd always been good
at making things up.

My tree listened
but soon enough
my eyes grew heavy,
limbs leaden from the drain
of being every thing for every one
except what I longed to be for me,
and the water below grew inviting
like a fitting place to sleep, to dream.

I shook myself awake enough
to climb down, relishing
the scratches on my limbs.
I hoped they'd bleed, tangible reasons
for this feeling of being flayed open.

35.

I'd barely taken a step
inside the cold stone walls
when this life came crashing back.

>   *Mistress!*

I'd seen the queen's lady's maid
but never exchanged a single word.
I could not fathom why she addressed me
as I headed toward my chambers.

Can I help you?

>   *No, I—*
>   *If only I could help you . . .*

Is the queen all right?

Even if she wasn't
I was not sure what
I could do.

>   *Oh, lady.*
>   *I shouldn't be the one*
>   *to tell you this, but*
>   *someone must*
>   *and I fear . . .*

Something had befallen Hamlet,
something worse than whatever
had already overthrown his mind.

The prince?

> *No, my lady.*
> *Your father.*
> *Your father is dead.*

[TRAP ROOM]

(Ophelia stops her tale, not because it has ended, but because the stoic girl is crying. Not full-on sobbing, wailing, nothing of the sort. Honestly, most people wouldn't notice the tear silently coursing its way down her cheek. Perhaps in a film, but not on a stage. Or in the trap room beneath one.

These girls are connected, though. They flowed from the quill of the same bard, after all. Ophelia hears the tear. Juliet, though enraptured by Ophelia's tale, also snaps her attention to the older girl.

Lavinia doesn't feel the impulse to comfort Cordelia. There's something about the girl that scares her, even now, vulnerable as she is.

No one can tell if Cordelia is locked inside her own world—her own memories bringing on the emotion—or if something in Ophelia's story unlocked her heart.)

SO YOUNG, MY LORD, AND TRUE

Division

When we were young, my father was inclined
to challenge us with puzzles and bestow
his favor on the one who solved them first.

Back then I was too small to stand a chance,
my sisters sharp and hungry for his praise
and I too young to understand the stakes.

But then one day the puzzle took the form
of checkered board and pieces all arranged
into an endgame we were bid to solve.

I noticed first the horses, tiny manes
exquisite, carved from stone and poised to charge
into a battle where they'd save the day.

When I reached for the shiny toy in awe
my eldest sister slapped my hand away.

> *You solve it in your head, you stupid girl.*

Sisters

My sisters were a pair, storm cloud and rain,
a bolt of lightning and a thunderclap.
Their little sister never could break in.
Their age was not what kept them out of reach,
nor competition for our father's praise.

It needled me, a child who craved regard.
What did they have that I would never know?
It's possible I bragged of Father's love,
a Joseph with my many-colored coat.

And so their bond encircled them so tight
that no one else ever could push inside.
Perhaps he never even favored me.
I'm just the only one who let him in.

Favor

He may have seen me as his favorite toy
but never did I dream what that could mean:
a better portion of his kingdom's lands
before he'd even left this earthly plain.

I thought he'd make arrangements with dear Kent,
sign documents that told us all his will,
and then one day upon his death we'd know.
To tell the truth, despite his mounting years
I never thought he'd leave this earth at all.

And on his death I'd hope for nothing more
than horse or castle. In my fondest dreams
command of soldiers who would serve the crown.
The property itself would best belong
to Goneril and Regan, and their men.
Their marriages allowed them both to rule
and make decisions no one would respect
unless they had the backing of a man.

And more than that, my sisters both possessed
a natural inclination toward the throne.

TRAP ROOM

(Cordelia, who has been distracted for the last few lines, stops abruptly with a sharp glance at Lavinia.

Without even realizing it, Lavinia had begun to tap out the rhythm of Cordelia's words with her feet. She never meant to interrupt. She'd give anything now to crash through this floor to whatever is beneath them, a terrifying thing to ponder, but not for Lavinia, who already faced every possible terror above, on the boards.

It's just that she felt the rhythm of the words, she connected with them, and they shook something loose inside her that escaped through her toes.

But now she shifts to sit on top of her feet. They'll go numb. She's survived worse.)

Goneril

The eldest daughter with the sharpest tongue
and eagle eye that tallied every score,
she'd cheat at games and always take the win.
So easy to assign her villainy.
It's harder if you look at how she grew
into a woman who could stand her ground.

Our mother died when she was just a child,
a sun eclipsed and never to emerge.
Just seven years of age, my sister mourned.
A mother would have changed things in her heart,
poor Goneril, who never felt the light
of Father's love, protection, or regard.

The middle sister, Regan, was her charge,
just five years old, and always at her side.
Her older sister sharpening her claws
at any hint of conflict in their path.
A wicked sense of humor too. And smart.

As I got old enough to overhear
discussions of our kingdom's politics
I marveled at the workings of her mind.
My oldest sister's views always expressed
but in a way that made my father think
he'd formed the thought all by his brilliant self.
And when she married, he was just the same;
her husband did her bidding unaware.

Regan

Then Regan learned from Goneril, but lacked
the same control, technique to master men.
Her temper flared at every little thing.
But also with her wit she'd send us all
into hysterics like we'd never known.
Her laugh was only sometimes cruel, I think.

She had her choice of husbands lining up
to have her hand, far more than Goneril.
Her beauty was one part of it, of course,
but more than that she burned a flame so bright
that moths galore were drawn to scorch their wings.
A trait she got from Father, I believe.

Injustice moved her more than anything,
the greatest being when her mother died
because a worthless baby took her life
        as she arrived without remorse or care.

Cordelia

They never said they blamed me for her death
but it's a fact our mother died when I
was brought into this world to take her place.

It made no sense that Father favored me
when I had wrenched away his love, his life.
He should despise me for the loss, and yet
he treated me as though I were a prize.

What's favor, anyway? It is not love.
It's expectation, pressure on a child
who feels the weight of memories unknown.

Eight Queens

I quickly learned the pieces and their moves,
solutions that would earn my father's praise

in constant conflict with my sisters' wrath
as little princess bested them each time.

Then came the day he brought to us a board
laid out with nothing on it but eight queens.

Eight queens to rule these squares of black and white,
but how to place them so they wouldn't war?

A joke to him, for chess without a king
was equal to a sky without a sun.

But I saw possibility, and more—
a chance to show the ruler I would be.

I shut my sisters out, invited queens
to dance their way across the board I kept

inside my mind where no one could intrude.
The dance concluded with each queen in place.

My sisters raged as I showed Father how
a kingdom ruled by women kept the peace.

[TRAP ROOM]

(In the trap room, Cordelia can't help but be aware of the very sisters she speaks of. For they're here, too.

They were raised by the same father. They have their own versions of these events. In their telling, Cordelia would be the fool who risked their father's wrath by taking his joke seriously. By suggesting women could not only rule, but do it better than men. Better than him.

Cordelia's sisters are the villains in most tellings of this story, and they have some things to say about that too.

Or they would if they were listening. They don't seem like they're listening. But then, sometimes it's hard to tell.)

Checkmate

Now I was grown, my sisters still a pair
when Father gathered us to hear his will.

Division of the kingdom not on death;
instead, an abdication of the throne.

Upon this board there stood a single king
who changed the rules mid-game and made it clear:

This was no abstract problem. He'd resolved
to split the kingdom up among his heirs.

My sisters had their husbands. Only I
would be entrusted with a sovereign rule.

heart in mouth, part 1

Oh, Father!
Could it be
you've been watching
all those times I thought
you didn't see me there,
soaking in the talk of strategy?

Could it be
you've seen me,
known I have the mind, the grit to lead?
I've learned the history, theories,
all those things you love
to debate with men
who've earned your respect?

> (Could it be
> I learned these things
> in order to win your respect?)

My sisters are cutthroat,
with husbands at their sides
but you could give them power
without abdicating your own.
This must be something different.
Am I a fool to dream
you might be handing me

the chance to shine?

Suitors

Of course he wouldn't let me rule alone;
two suitors for my hand were ushered in:
the Duke of Burgundy; the King of France.

I never dreamed of love; I know my place.
A marriage is political for all
but royalty must make this choice with care.
My only hope: a match to keep the peace.

The Duke of Burgundy was shrewd and sharp;
perhaps a bit too much like Goneril
for me to ever feel respect and warmth.
But marriage wasn't for my comfort, so
I'd take him if my father thought him fit.

The King of France was softer, watchful, kind.
But I knew better than to trust his show.
A person cannot rule a land without
a mastery of cunning and control.
Still, his was smooth, a balm to calm us all.

But either way, there'd be a man to guide
my hand in every choice I'd ever make.

The Problem

The problem Father laid before us was

> *Declare how much you love your father-king.*
> *Depending on your answer I'll decide*
> *your portion of the kingdom and its lands.*
> *I'll abdicate the throne and spend my days*
> *admiring all three daughters, rightful heirs.*

> *But careful how you speak, for if I think*
> *your love for me is less than I deserve*
> *I'll give the lands more bountiful to one*
> *who lays before me all the love I'm owed.*

But no one stopped him, called it all absurd.
And no one questioned how he'd judge our love.
I saw not one exchange of worried looks.
I turned to Kent, beloved confidant,
so sure he'd point out flaws within this plan.
T'was imprecise, subjective, and betrayed
expected norms of all we'd ever learned.

Divisions must be based on age or else
another way to measure, black and white.
And more than that I wished for Kent to say
that Father was advanced in age but not
quite ready to completely leave the throne.
Why abdicate at all while he was still
quite capable of rule (and cunning games)?
But Kent said nothing, loyal even still.

First Goneril would speak, the eldest child.
She wore a mask, but then she always did.
This one was painted with the love she bore
for Father and his throne and all the lands,
her heart devoted to his every care,
her greed so naked that I filled with shame.

Then Regan next—she didn't disappoint.
And classic Regan started with high praise
for Goneril, such pretty words she said;
but then the knife she twisted, raised the stakes
and claimed her sister fell too short of love.
Our Regan wore no mask; she never did.
Her greed on full display, her motives clear.

My father would not stand such avarice.
He'd tell us that he played us all along
and they revealed themselves to be without
the judgment that a ruler must possess.

But then he turned to me and it was clear
this all unfolded just as he had planned.
My sisters played the parts he'd given them
and now I had to dance before the crowds.
The grand finale of my love, his goal,
while I resisted stepping on the stage.

TRAP ROOM

(A moment here, a suspended breath. Every single woman in this labyrinth knows Cordelia will make it onto the stage. For what other choice does she have? They've all done it, performed their parts night after night, even when they've felt like nothing more than marionettes whose limbs are jerked by an unseen hand.

Lavinia returns to the stage each time, knowing the brutality that awaits. If there was another path, she'd take it.

But even knowing this, they're in suspense. For that's the power of the story. Even when they know how it will turn out, there's the spark of hope that this time might be different.

Possibility.)

My Dance

The favored daughter never truly got
unmitigated love and pure respect.
Attention and rewards, yes, praise galore.
His wrath directed somewhere else, perhaps
(including when I might have done the deed).

But it was all external, all a show
that he was capable of love, a mask
of who he knew the world would want to see.
Perhaps it's what's expected of a king,
a constant expectation to perform.

He told me that I'm beautiful and smart.
He never asked me who I really am.
He told me that I'll make a goodly wife.
He never asked me what I want to be.
He told me who he is and what he wants
and I'd reflect, absorb, and deify.

The fact that I could see his truest self
and know it's flawed and ugly at the core
did not reveal a lack of love for him.
In fact, I loved him so my heart would break
each time I realized that he never would
return the love I bore him with his heart.

The fact I loved him didn't mean I could
articulate it like the price of grain.
To do so would diminish my true love

apparent in my grace for him through years.
My love displayed by growing into one
who owned her thoughts and choices even when
to do so put in jeopardy her life.

To falsely flatter would not show my love
so when he said my turn had come to speak
I said
                    nothing.

heart in mouth, part 2

Your words:

> *Nothing comes of nothing.*
> *Speak again.*

This moment is the one
you choose to bid me speak?
If I should count the times
you've asked to hear my voice,
I come up with

nothing.

Nothing comes of nothing.
Speak again.

But now that it suits you,
now that you want my words
to stroke your ego,
I should speak again.
I should tell you
what you want to hear
in precisely
the way
you want
to hear it
or I am useless to you.

You haven't seen me,
have no idea who I am,
how I could take this land
and make it great. Imagine
if I'd had a father,
mentor, guiding me.

I won't dance for you.
I won't contort my true devotion
into a playing piece
upon your board.
I love you.

I love you more than you deserve
       (for that's not why we love).

But I won't rip my heart out
for you to devour, leaving nothing
for myself.

Thunder and Lightning

As Father's rage began and built with haste,
the masks around the table fell away.
My sisters gasped, but didn't take my side.
Their husbands looked on, wary, buttoned-up.

Dear Kent did try to stop my father from
unleashing words he might regret, except
then Father's words advanced on Kent as well.
The Duke of Burgundy and King of France
observed the scene, the match they meant to make.
Should they ally themselves with such a king,
so volatile, so careless with his kin?

But there'd be no alliance here it seemed
for Father made it clear the price I'd pay
for failing to perform my given role.
I'd be cut off, and banished, and disowned.

I barely heard the voices all around.
This couldn't be and yet I'd always known
there'd come an end to being Father's pet.
That moment came and I could not escape
the feeling of a thing quite like relief.

Dowry

My father spoke to Burgundy and France
as though I were a passing cloud, mere air.
They came to take my hand (and power, lands)
but would they want me now that I had none?

I looked not at my sisters, couldn't bear
to see upon their faces the delight
I knew they'd feel to see their sister fall.

The Duke of Burgundy was absolute.
Without the land I wasn't what he thought;
he'd take his leave without another word.
The King of France would say the same, I thought,
but in a gentler way; he'd burn no bridge.

Instead, he came to stand at my right hand
and told me that I had a home with him.
I had no time to parse his purpose then
but knew he wouldn't take me without cause.

Cold comfort to take refuge in a land
beside a man with motives undisclosed,
but better that than wander lost, alone.

Goodbyes

My father raged that I had not been left
defenseless, homeless, lost upon the moors.
He stormed away, the rest of us in shock.

My sister's husbands hurried to his aid;
their wives had not a word to bolster me.
But France's hand was gentle on my arm.

> *You might not see your sisters after this.*
> *Would you prefer to leave without goodbyes?*

I was not even sure they'd care if I
should leave their company forever now.
Perhaps they wouldn't notice my withdrawal
but I would know I'd given up the chance
to be a sister to them one last time.

They looked on me with scorn as I approached.
They could not mourn a sister when their hearts
were focused on the wealth that they had gained.

I wish you well. I won't forget you both.

A smile would crack the mask that Goneril wore.
She nodded, turned away without a word.

Our father—please look after him for me.
I didn't mean to cause him such distress.

Then Regan spoke, her words like sharpest knives.

>   *Don't tell us what to do with him. We're more*
>   *aware of what our duty obligates*
>   *than you, who shun him with a heart of ice.*

Had I been blind? Did both my sisters play
this twisted game, not for their private gain
but for this land? Devotion to the crown?
Was I a fool to see myself as one
who made a sacrifice born out of love?

heart in mouth, part 3

Dear Father,
dear Britannia,
dear only home I've ever known,
dear Mother who departed before I could draw
    breath

I did everything you asked me,
became the girl you formed
and for my pains I'm foreign, reviled.

It's cruel, even for you.

Safe Travels

The ship and I unmoored upon the waves,
the winds were harsh, the water menacing.
France joined me at the prow to brave the storm.

> *Do tell me, please, Cordelia if I*
> *can help to ease your grief in any way?*

The tears that sprung up instantly did not
reflect the queen I meant to be and so
I tried to play them off as ocean spray.
I dashed them from my cheeks, but could not speak.

> *I understand I cannot give you back*
> *your father or the lands you should have had—*

I truly do not care about the lands.

He kept his peace, allowed me dignity.

> *Since this is now the life that you must live*
> *I hope you'll tell me if there's anything*
> *that we could do to make you comfortable.*

I marveled how he didn't race to fill
the space between us with more useless words.
A tactic I had never seen before,
with Father as my model for a king.

But king he was, regardless of his ease.
He could not give me what did not exist:

> a father's love, a mother's life,
> and sisters
> who would wipe away my tears.

Black Knight

I learned
what my sisters
thought of tears
the same day I learned
not to best my father.

After I placed the eight queens in harmony
he began to summon me for games.
My sisters lingered, made excuses
to draw near the board, but
they had not been invited
to play.

He never held back, the king's game
a war in miniature, and he the ruthless
    conqueror.
I never minded losing, though, for we all knew
I'd won his attention, and there was no higher
    prize.

What I didn't realize was my sisters only lurked
because they knew how this would end
and they would be there when it did.

The day my black knight
checkmated his white king,
my father packed up his board
and never played with me again.

Land Legs

Off the ship
and onto French soil
I felt no steadier,
each step on shifting sand,
each word foreign on my tongue.

The king had me escorted to my chambers
and I believed I'd barely see his face
until the necessary functions were required.

But the next day
he appeared at my door
with food and wine
and gleaming box
tucked beneath his arm.

> *May I come in?*

It was his castle
and what's more, my stomach growled.
I stepped aside.

Hungry as I was, my eyes
were pulled from the plate of bread and cheese
to the box, which unfolded to reveal
an exquisite battalion of chess pieces
carved from ebony and ivory.

My hand reached for a knight
and no one slapped it away.

La Reine

He offered me
the advantage of white.
I declined.

Each movement strategic
we advanced across the board.
Everything else in this land
was foreign, but la reine
was as powerful as a queen,
pawns as underestimated as les pions.

Strategy always interested me more
than weapons, overwhelming force.
No one was going to teach the princess
how to wield a sword, but my mind
could be as finely honed
as the best of the king's advisors.

The more I listened in
as a girl in the corner
I marveled at how often
the strategies I silently crafted
mirrored those presented by the men
in Father's war room.

In this strange place, a different king before me,
I wondered if my invented strategies
might be welcomed.

But not now.
For I was two moves away
from besting him.

A Gift

The king with his chessboard
was not an anomaly.
Each person I met
in the court of France
extended similar kindness.

But unfamiliar as I was
with generosity and welcome,
I could not say what was real
and what was calculated.

As well as daily games of strategy,
the king gave me a wedding gift:
a glorious horse I named Pion.
France saw my need for freedom,
took me out for hours until I knew
the lands enough to roam them on my own.

As I rode, my brain cleared
of clinging ghosts.
I didn't trust the king, not fully,
but took small steps
to take him at his word.

Each time I rode, I'd break
the bonds that should have nurtured me
but left me skeptical of love.
The pain had served its purpose,
protected me, reminded me to be on guard.
But it would not serve me any longer.

At least that's what I thought until
France met me in the stables,
a stricken look upon his face.
My heart still pounded from my thrilling ride,
but at his face, I sobered.

What is it? What is wrong?

                    Your father-king.

Betrayal

My sisters
slammed their doors
in Father's face
the moment we sailed away.

Our sources reported
that troops approached,
but under whose command
they couldn't say.
The only sure thing:
His daughters were to blame.

All the bonds I'd untied
astride Pion reknit themselves
around my heart.

What am I to do from here?

> *Every French knight and rook and bishop*
> *is yours to command.*

> *And king as well.*

PART TWO

Nothing will come of nothing:
speak again.

—Cordelia's father, Act 1, Scene 1

You speak like a green girl.

—Ophelia's father, Act 1, Scene 3

Speak not, reply not,
do not answer me.

—Juliet's father, Act 3, Scene 5

And, with thy shame,
thy father's sorrow die.

—Lavinia's father, Act 5, Scene 3

(In the trap room, there is a pause. An intermission, if you will.

Perhaps it's intermission up above too, the spectators already forgetting the women who've played their parts and then melted away, leaving the men to their glory. The audience stretches, unwraps candy, checks their phones. Goes in search of the restroom. Time stops inside the theater, but outside, it goes on. Messages come in.

"Sorry, just got this. I'm at a play," they write back.

The women of the trap room need a moment with Cordelia's story, and the cliffhanger she's left them on. Many can relate to being forced into a marriage they wouldn't have chosen. She's not the only one who's summoned troops—the one who eternally reeks of ashes has turned her ear to better hear a familiar tale—and she's definitely not the only one to have defied her father.

But none have summoned troops to defend the father who disowned them. Is this strength, or weakness? Is she only running back in an attempt to grovel for the favor of a man who'll surely strike her down again? Or is she stronger than any of them could ever fathom?

Of course Juliet is the first to speak. Famously impulsive, but also unafraid to sound silly, which is a quality few of these women have.)

JULIET

I have a question?

CORDELIA

Oh. We're talking now?

> *(Braver than anyone could fathom, maybe, but Cordelia probably wouldn't have told her tale if she'd known there'd be a Q & A afterward.)*

JULIET

I mean, did you just tell us all that and then expect us to sit in silence for eternity?

CORDELIA

Is that still on the table?

OPHELIA

I don't mind answering questions.

JULIET

Oh, good! I have questions for you too. But first—

(She turns to Cordelia.)

CORDELIA

How did my new husband trust me with command of his troops when he barely knew me?

JULIET

No, that made sense. I'd follow you into battle.

OPHELIA

He is very nice.

CORDELIA

Yes.
(Pause.)
I'm not a mind reader.

JULIET

Oh! Right! Sorry!

Why'd you tell it like that? All . . . singsongy?

CORDELIA

Singsongy?

OPHELIA

I think she means the rhythm.

CORDELIA

The iambic pentameter?

                              JULIET

Whatever it's called.

> *(Lavinia taps out the rhythm with her feet, and the other girls nod*
> *along.)*

                            CORDELIA

It elevates the language. Gives it a structure. Plus, the rhythm mimics the
human heartbeat, which helps the speaker or the audience connect—

                              JULIET

Those are the Bard's reasons. Not yours.

> *(Beat.)*

                            CORDELIA

You don't know my reasons.

                              JULIET

That's why I'm asking.

> *(Pause.)*

                            CORDELIA

I guess . . . I like structure.

                              JULIET

No kidding.

                             OPHELIA

Predictability?

                            CORDELIA

Not in a boring way.

                              JULIET

I don't know. I think maybe that structure kind of needs performers to
breathe life into it.

CORDELIA

Are you saying my story is lifeless?

JULIET

Harder to connect to.

OPHELIA

Maybe that's not the structure. Maybe it's just her.

CORDELIA

Thank you?

JULIET

I guess all I'm saying is maybe you could open it up a little. Invite us in more.

OPHELIA

She did a few times. With her heart in her mouth—

CORDELIA

Don't talk about that.

OPHELIA

Sorry.

JULIET

And once you left your father's court! It changed then too, right?

(Cordelia doesn't answer. She hadn't made this connection. Juliet turns to Lavinia, the rhythm keeper, who gives the tiniest of nods.)

(Beat.)

JULIET

I'm not trying to hurt your feelings.

CORDELIA

Please. You saw what my family's like.

OPHELIA

Yeah, your dad. Wow.

*(Lavinia snorts, barely audible. Their fathers—with their impotent
name-calling, their feeble narcissism—have nothing on hers.)*

JULIET

Here's what I don't get. How they could turn on us so quickly. Our own
fathers.

CORDELIA

Oh, you sweet summer child.

OPHELIA

Yours did call you some terrible names.

JULIET

There were more! I didn't even tell you! Mistress minion, green-sickness
carrion! Tallow-face? I mean, thanks a lot!

CORDELIA

Did he curse your womb to shrivel up?

JULIET

Okay, no. Did yours?

CORDELIA

Not *my* womb.
(She glances toward her eldest sister's corner.)
She'd told him he couldn't stay at her house, so. To me he just said he'd
rather I was a savage who eats its own children.

(Beat.)

OPHELIA

Um.

JULIET

I was also a hilding; a wretched puling fool; a disobedient wretch—

OPHELIA

What even is a hilding?

CORDELIA

I was a wretch too. Right before he said it would have been better for me not to be born than to offend him.

OPHELIA

I'm starting to be grateful my father was just kind of condescending.

JULIET

A whining mammet!

CORDELIA (to Ophelia)

Yours never turned on you because you never did anything.

JULIET

Harsh.

OPHELIA

What do you mean?

CORDELIA

I mean she and I both stood up to our fathers. Mine was for a good reason. Integrity, et cetera. But it's almost worse that Juliet's freaked out when she was just a lovesick kid.

JULIET

You're not that much older than I am.

CORDELIA

I'm a lot more mature.

(JULIET sticks out her tongue.)

CORDELIA

(. . .)

JULIET

Okay, fair.

OPHELIA

I did things.

CORDELIA

Did you? Name one.

(Pause.)

JULIET

I'm really sorry, but she's kind of right. He told you not to see the prince anymore, so you stopped. And then he used you to spy on Hamlet and you let him. And then you just sat there at the play while Hamlet said all that gross stuff.

CORDELIA

You were spineless, so your father never had a reason to turn on you.

OPHELIA

What was I supposed to do? Get myself kicked out? That worked great for you two, huh?

CORDELIA

There you go, growing a little tiny bit of spine. Like a . . .
a hummingbird spine.

OPHELIA

Hummingbirds are incredibly strong.

CORDELIA

Then I take it back.

JULIET

She doesn't mean to be cruel—

CORDELIA

Excuse me, but I am extremely on the record as not wanting words put into my mouth.

JULIET

She's just answering my question about how my dad could go from, like, adoring father to saying I'd rot in the streets if I didn't do what he said. And it's because I said no. Same as she did.

OPHELIA

So those are the choices? Have an opinion and get disowned, or bow to their every wish?

CORDELIA

Basically.

JULIET

It's not only having an opinion. You have to express it.
   (Beat.)
But hey! At least you and I got to experience love.

CORDELIA

For like five minutes.

OPHELIA

I don't even know if I did.

JULIET

I think you did. Your Hamlet was a complex guy. I mean I'm not qualified to diagnose mental health stuff, but there's definitely something going on there. And then his father dies and his mom immediately gets remarried to his uncle?! That would mess with anyone's abilities to have a healthy relationship.

CORDELIA

He treated her like shit. Mental health stuff doesn't excuse that.

JULIET

True.

CORDELIA

And your "love"? Pfft.

JULIET

I'm sorry, our names are synonymous with *love story*. You don't even need our whole names—just our initials. R and J. You look up *love story* in the dictionary and you get, like, a picture of the balcony scene.

CORDELIA

Ah yes, that took place . . . consults notes . . . the day you first laid eyes on each other?

JULIET

It's called love at first sight. Ever heard of it?

CORDELIA

Lust at first sight, more like.

JULIET

No. No! I mean, yes, but also no. I hate this take, that we were just stupid teenagers, that we didn't know what love was, that it was too fast. Were we impulsive? Sure. Were our hormones raging? I mean obviously. Have you seen Romeo?

But we both made choices, sacrifices. I stood up to what my entire culture expected of me. Would I have done that just for horniness? Romeo could have had any girl he wanted, one who wouldn't cause a war and get him banished. We were both willing to take huge risks for love. And not only love for each other. For our families. We were both willing to risk being cut off forever on the chance that our love might blossom into peace for all Verona.

                          OPHELIA

I think it's romantic.

                          CORDELIA

Of course you do.

                          OPHELIA

It wasn't so sudden for me. I didn't believe the prince would even look
at me. I wouldn't have dared to love him, though I did think he was the
most beautiful boy I had ever seen.

                          CORDELIA

Gag me.

                          JULIET

You're just jealous.

                          CORDELIA

You know what? That's offensive. Not everyone's into romance. Or sex.

                          OPHELIA

But everyone wants to be loved, don't they?

                          CORDELIA

Well.

   (Silence.)

                          OPHELIA

Do you think they're capable of it?

                          JULIET

What, love?

                          CORDELIA

Who?

                          OPHELIA

Men, I guess. Fathers. But not just fathers.

JULIET

Romeo was.

CORDELIA

As a horny teenager.

I'm not saying it wasn't real, just that it was . . . new. But what if things had turned out differently? Your ridiculous plan actually worked and you're five, ten, twenty years into marriage. What then? Is he still climbing your trellis to sing your praises?

OPHELIA

Comfortable love is still love. My parents had it.

CORDELIA

Yes, but Romeo. You have to admit, he was a changeable guy. He went into that ball swooning over your friend Rosaline—

JULIET

I never liked her.

CORDELIA

—and came out recklessly in love with you. Do you really believe he'd never change again, turn toward someone else? Betray you.

JULIET

Who hurt you?

OPHELIA

I mean . . . her dad?

CORDELIA

Super helpful, thanks.

OPHELIA

But Cordelia, your France seemed really loyal. Genuine.

CORDELIA

Yeah, but marriage—

OPHELIA & JULIET

"—is political."

JULIET

You seriously lucked out with that one, though.

OPHELIA

It's not an epic romance like Juliet's, but I think it's a love story all the same.

CORDELIA

You don't think it's suspicious?

OPHELIA

What?

CORDELIA

How he took me when I brought nothing to the marriage.

JULIET

You brought yourself.

CORDELIA

That's not the way these things work.

OPHELIA

What if it is, though? What if you, a strong, smart partner, were enough for him?

(Lavinia snorts and Cordelia notices her for the first time. Really notices her. Acknowledges her. They exchange a look, a rolling of the eyes at the naïveté of these girls who've suffered, but not in the very specific way they have, fathers willing to blot them from the record the moment their existence became inconvenient.)

JULIET

Wow, okay. Don't mind us being nice and supportive.

CORDELIA

Spare me nice.

OPHELIA

I think she was just raised to believe certain things. About herself. And others.

JULIET

And having feelings.

CORDELIA

I have feelings, okay! Big, dramatic ones, even! Do you want me to rend my garments and sob?

JULIET

I mean, if that's what you're feeling . . .

OPHELIA

I think love is just hard, for everyone. It's hard if you wear it on your sleeve and it's hard if you bottle it up.

(Cordelia zeroes in on Lavinia. It's not that she wants to deflect the focus off herself, although she does. But now that she's noticed Lavinia, really noticed her, she wants to know who this girl is, this girl who somehow understands her, for all their differences.)

CORDELIA

What's your story?

(Lavinia looks over her shoulder, unable to believe Cordelia is speaking to her. Anyone is speaking to her.)

CORDELIA

Yes, you. Do you wear it on your sleeve, or bottle it up?

(Lavinia opens her mouth and the girls flinch as some blood trickles out. Instinct sends her arm flying to cover her mouth with a hand that's not there, leaving her more exposed than ever. It's too much. She shakes them off, shrinks back.

Cordelia, Ophelia, and Juliet exchange glances. Even some of the other women are watching from their corners. It's uncomfortable. No one wants to face whatever's happened to this girl. They realize this is uncharitable. It's just that they all have their own stuff to deal with, and hers is more obviously traumatic, but why do we have to compare?

Plus, their shared horror over her wounds has brought them together in a rare moment of mutual understanding, but that excludes her even further. Which is gross.

Still, when Ophelia speaks, it's not that she's greedy for the spotlight. She's just trying to give Lavinia the shadows she seems to want.)

OPHELIA

So . . . do you really think Hamlet loved me?

JULIET

I do. Of course I do. Those letters he wrote you? I mean, come on!

OPHELIA (*to Cordelia*)

What about you?

CORDELIA

Me?

OPHELIA

Do you think Hamlet loved me? You can be honest.

JULIET

But not cruel.

(Pause.)

CORDELIA

I think he did. In his way. For a time. I think if things had been different . . . if his father hadn't died and broken his heart, and he hadn't killed your father and broken your heart, but that's the thing, isn't it? There are always these insurmountable hurdles because we don't love in a bubble—we love in the world—and I'm just not sure love is possible with everything conspiring against it.

JULIET

But you managed to love your father. In the world.

CORDELIA

And somehow still broke his heart. And mine.

OPHELIA

I guess there's a reason they're called tragedies.

(*Silence.*)

CORDELIA

Tragedies or comedies. Either everybody dies or everybody marries.

JULIET

That's kind of messed up.

OPHELIA

Not everybody dies.

CORDELIA

Your father, your brother, your boyfriend, his mother, his uncle—

OPHELIA

Okay.

(*Pause.*)

OPHELIA

There's also the histories and the problem plays.

CORDELIA

The histories are just what happened. But the problem plays . . . they're somewhere in the middle between tragedy and comedy, and somehow that makes them problematic?

OPHELIA

That's not what the name means. Problem plays. They're about ethical problems.

CORDELIA

Really?

OPHELIA

Anyway, the Bard didn't call them that. It was some scholar.

CORDELIA

Oh.

(Pause.)

JULIET

So, are we going to talk about your sisters?

CORDELIA

Whose? Mine?

(Cordelia glances at her sisters in their corners.)

OPHELIA

I only have a brother.

CORDELIA

What about them?

JULIET

Don't you think they get kind of shafted?

CORDELIA

I mean . . . it's a tragedy. Pretty much everyone does.

JULIET

No, but I mean. Even the way you tell it. They're cruel and cunning and bordering on monstrous.

CORDELIA

You should try playing chess with them.

OPHELIA

Devil's advocate here—

CORDELIA

Am I the devil?

OPHELIA

They do gouge out a man's eyes and cheat on their husbands and kill each other, basically.

CORDELIA

Thank you.

JULIET

That's not great. But before that. Even when you were growing up, you make them sound so awful. Just because you were left out or whatever. Boo-hoo.

Have you ever thought about what made them like that?

CORDELIA

Of course I have.

JULIET

Like, the way your dad turned on you at the end. Maybe he'd been treating them like that all along. What would that do to a person?

OPHELIA

Hopefully not make them gouge out someone's eyes.

JULIET

But that's not what I'm talking about. That was the Bard's choice. Convenient for women to be pure or mad or evil.

CORDELIA

What else is there?

JULIET

That's what I'm asking. What else is there? What else were they? And
did they deserve to not only die like they did, but then have their dead
bodies brought back out onstage as a spectacle?

CORDELIA

You're one to talk about dead bodies on the stage. *"Oh, woe is me, my life's
so sad the only possible solution is to take a potion that will make my family
believe I'm dead, parade my body to a crypt, and leave it displayed like a
monument to teenage stupidity!"*

(Beat.)

OPHELIA

You can be really mean.

CORDELIA

Making up for a lifetime of biting my tongue, I guess.
(Beat.)
I'm sorry.

JULIET

Anyway, she's right.

CORDELIA

I am?

JULIET

Not about the teenage stupidity. That's still a garbage take. But the bodies
on the stage. What is with that? You die offstage, but your father brings
your corpse back onstage and uses it as a . . .

CORDELIA

A prop.

JULIET

Right, a prop! It's, like, this thing that gives him his great moment to shine.

OPHELIA

I die offstage too.

JULIET

Right! At least most productions don't bring your body back onstage, but there's a whole big scene about digging your grave—with clowns, by the way—and then your brother and the prince both get to have their scenery-chewing moments of throwing their bodies into the grave with you. You might not be on the stage, but your body is still this thing for them to use.

CORDELIA

Plus there's all the art.

OPHELIA

What?

CORDELIA

The art. There's, like, tons of paintings of you dead in the water. Like that's the only way to remember you. The perfect woman, finally silent.

JULIET

Also like drowning isn't a horrible, violent death.

OPHELIA

It really, really is.

(Pause.)

CORDELIA

It's frightening. Being used like that. Lear is an old man. Being hauled around, limp, completely at the mercy of someone focused on the defining performance of their lifetime . . .

JULIET

It's vulnerable. Do you know how long I have to lie there, knowing eyes are on me every second? And once I get to the crypt, I have to stay there, vulnerable, all through Romeo's laments, and his fight with Paris, praying they don't misstep and slam into me, all through his death—

OPHELIA

I've always wondered . . .

JULIET

What?

OPHELIA

When you wake and find him, dead, do you ever stop to think, before you plunge the dagger into your own heart?

JULIET

Think what.

OPHELIA

I mean. Do you think of living instead? Do you think of what he would want for you in that moment? Or think of your parents?

JULIET

Did you?

OPHELIA

Both my parents were dead already.

(Silence.)

JULIET

I guess I don't. Because really, there's no other choice in that moment. I've defied my father, married his enemy, faked my death. Do you think I could just show up at Casa di Capulet all "Just kidding, I'm back! Is Paris still up for that wedding?"

CORDELIA

There's always another choice.

OPHELIA

Is there?

CORDELIA

Of course there is! You could have stayed out of that tree, for starters! Juliet could have told her parents sooner that she'd married Romeo. I could have . . .

OPHELIA

Told your father what he wanted to hear?

JULIET

Of course we have choices, but you make it sound like if we were just smarter, then the entire patriarchal systems built up around us wouldn't be able to hold us back. Sometimes you make all the right choices and shitty things still happen.

CORDELIA

Believe me, I know.

(Silence.)

JULIET

But now you have me thinking.

CORDELIA

Oh no.

JULIET

For argument's sake . . . if you got to set the stage for your own story—

CORDELIA

But we don't. That's the whole point. We flow from his pen and here we are.

JULIET

I refuse to accept that. He didn't even create us. I was lifted from an English poem lifted from an Italian monk. Hamlet's based on an earlier play, which is based on a history of Denmark. And Lear—

CORDELIA

I know. Leir of Britain.

But the Bard's versions—

JULIET

Which bard?

(Pause.)

CORDELIA

What?

JULIET

Which bard? You say "the Bard" like everyone knows exactly who you mean—

CORDELIA & OPHELIA

They do.

JULIET

But a bard is just a poet, a minstrel, a storyteller. If we're specific, he's the Bard of Avon, but probably there've been other bards in Avon who have some thoughts on that.

CORDELIA

Fine, yes, but his are the ones that have lasted. He chose and elevated the stories he knew would resonate. And here we are.

JULIET

Simple as that.

CORDELIA

I'm not saying it was simple, but . . .

JULIET

Look at it this way. When he was writing these stories, he was shaking them up. Telling them his way. He had no way to know his versions would be the ones still told four hundred years later.

CORDELIA

I mean, he was a white man. He might have had an inkling.

OPHELIA

But there were lots of other white men telling versions that didn't last.

JULIET

Exactly! Thank you!

What if we dared to have that kind of confidence? What if we dared to tell our versions as though we knew they'd last, we believed they'd be the ones people would hear for centuries to come?

(*Cordelia still looks deeply skeptical. But Ophelia's into it. Juliet can see that.*)

JULIET

Ophelia, if you could change your story, what would be different?

OPHELIA

My mother wouldn't die.

JULIET

How would that change things? Let's say she lived. Does that mean you'd never meet the prince? Probably not, if your father stayed on his course to advisor.

OPHELIA

I think having her there to help me understand Hamlet would have changed things for me. But maybe not for him.

CORDELIA

This is pointless. Her mother didn't live. She can't change that.

JULIET

You're the one who was all "make different choices"!

CORDELIA

But you can't choose for a parent not to die!

JULIET

Let's say you can. Forget the Bard. Let's say Hamlet's uncle still kills his father and marries his mother because, first of all, a story needs conflict and also life is messy, right?

CORDELIA

I would like to be on the record that this is stupid.

JULIET

Forget her. What would you change?

(All eyes are on Ophelia. This is unprecedented. A chance to tell it again, her way? She's always thought there was only one way this story could play out. It was written by the Bard, all those years ago, and ever since then, she's been loving and losing and drowning beautifully and then crashing through the stage. Over and over again. It's muscle memory. It's horrible, but there's a comfort in the inevitability of it all.

This chance now? It's deeply unsettling. And so full of promise.)

PART THREE

Move thy tongue,
For silence is a sign of discontent.

—Elizabeth Cary
The Tragedy of Mariam, 1613

FARE YOU WELL, MY DOVE

1.

Mother insists
we keep our cottage in the village
when Father becomes advisor to the new king.

We can't live there,
for Father must be close at hand
as the new king rules a grieving kingdom.

But we return to the cottage often,
Mother and I, to visit with neighbors,
share their griefs and joys.

Mother brings herbs and flowers
from the castle's gardens
to make balms and tinctures
that she shares with all she can.

On our return to the castle one day
a royal carriage passes us by.

      The prince has returned.

Mother's voice is tender.
She was young when she lost her parents.
No doubt she's already concocting
a balm to soothe his grieving soul.

2.

My heart leaps at his return,
as does my shame. He's here
because his father died.

But I'm glad he's back,
my jolly audience,
tree companion,
brightest light in all the castle.

When he climbs down
from the carriage, though,
his eyes are dark.
They flicker my way
without recognition.

Mother puts an arm around me.

> *Come, Ophelia.*
> *He's had a difficult journey.*

3.

His journey will only
grow more difficult.
I know I can't understand.
I've never lost a loved one.

Many have died
under Mother's care.
I've held hands as souls
passed on, cradled babies
born blue as jays.
But never someone
I love with all my heart.

When he finally meets me at our tree
I hold him as he cries. His tears
water the daisies I planted.

       They grow.

4.

Don't leave me.

We stumble together
to his chambers.
It isn't proper
but he can't bear
the prying eyes
on his every move.
I understand.

I won't.

The door thuds shut
behind us and his lips
crash into mine.
He wants to bury himself
inside me to hide
from the world.

I want that too.
His absence starved me,
a flower without her sun
and I desire the hottest day
to scorch my petals.

I want him
and I want my body
to be a shield, covering his grief,
even if I can give him only moments

where he thinks not on his pain
but on his pleasure.

I want these things,
but also I know
his mind is not his own,
and while the rest of court
might think only on my virtue,
I will think on his.

Let me hold you.
I'll tell you a story
of a boy and a girl
who weather a storm
and then build a home
made of daisies.

5.

He's angry at first.
I've denied him, a prince,
and a grieving one at that.

He's always offered
his every whim,
the palace clamoring
to anticipate his needs.
But I'm different.

6.

With time
he still grieves
but he's closer to the boy
who danced upon a branch.
We speak of love, desire,
what we each need.

In his chambers, curtains drawn,
there's nothing in the world but
　　　　his hands on my skin
　　　　my skin on his pounding pulse
fumbling awkwardness and laughter
abandoned as a rhythm builds
until we both cry out, wrapped
around each other,
us against the world.

I slip back to my chambers,
dandelion clock upon the breeze.
He may not be mine forever
but he is mine for now.

[TRAP ROOM]

(Ophelia pauses, unsure if she's said too much. Unsure if it's all right to tell a story where her desire, her pleasure matter.

But everyone's listening, nodding. Even Cordelia.)

CORDELIA

Why'd you stop?

OPHELIA

I wasn't sure . . .

JULIET

You seemed sure.

OPHELIA

But I wasn't sure I should say it.

JULIET

It's part of your story.

OPHELIA

Yes, but . . .
    (She glances toward Cordelia.)
Not everyone's comfortable hearing about it.

CORDELIA

It's not my story.

JULIET

Keep going!

OPHELIA

Really?

(Lavinia draws a touch closer. She's not sure there's a version of her own story that could ever include desire or pleasure. But it's comforting to know it can happen. For some people. She pierces Ophelia with her gaze, her want to hear what's next.)

7.

The next day
he does not meet me
at our tree.

Or the next.

When finally I see him
his eyes gleam,
unrecognizable.

> It's nothing to do with you.

His friend Horatio tells me
not to bother him,
not to be so touchy.
The prince has more important things
on his mind than a silly girl.

Could he have used me
and disposed of me so easily?
Not before. But maybe now
for grief has turned him inside out.

My heart cracks,
a branch that will snap off
if the smallest bug
should light upon it.

8.

Time does not
strengthen the branch,
only starves it
of what it requires.

One night Hamlet appears
in my chambers, clothes and hair askew,
saying nothing, grasping me
too tight and staring into my eyes
so disturbed and frightening
that I go to my father
the very next day.

I know he will scold me
for involving myself with the prince
but getting help matters more.

Father doesn't scold, though.
Instead reports to King Claudius
that Hamlet's antics are due to love.

That isn't what I said—

But they don't listen.
They want the easy explanation,
want me to pose as their doll
and stage a conversation with the prince
that they can watch for proof,
a way to absolve themselves
of his desperate pain and need.

I won't.

9.

I won't
be used
without consent.

You think me
easy to ignore.
Perhaps I am.

But only notice me
when you have use
and I will scream
so loud I'll wake the dead,
and they might have
some words for you.

10.

When I hear there'll be a play,
I think for a moment
my Hamlet is back.

At least the tiniest glimpse,
the boy who found solace in stories
and healing in shared emotion.

For he has invited the players,
rallied the court to attend, a thing
his father often did, but not his uncle-king.

I'm not surprised when he spurns his mother,
angry she married so quickly,
angry she chose her husband's brother.

I am surprised when he not only
bids me sit with him but sprawls on the ground,
head in my lap, a position we've shared
only in the gardens, his chambers,
my hands in his hair, my stories
weaving his grief into flower crowns.

I look to my parents.
Mother frowns; Father shrugs
as if to say, *Stay. It's fine.*

It isn't fine when Hamlet says
filthy things for all to hear

all the while sprawled in my lap
so close to where we've made each other
sigh with pleasure, release our pain.

The play is strange
and I barely notice,
for Hamlet's commentary
is far more shocking.
When the king storms out
I'm so relieved he made it stop.

Hamlet is delighted; I've no idea why.
But now that his head is out of my lap,
his mouth is done running
and the court is no longer
trained on our every move,
I'm furious.

He and Horatio stand together,
agitated, talking as though planning a battle.
I try to catch his eye. I know he sees
but chooses to ignore me.

I need to talk to you.

    He's busy.

Horatio dismisses me
though Hamlet is right there.

I don't care.

This time the prince stops
and looks at me,
but he's distracted again
as Gertrude sweeps past.

      Later, Ophelia.
      I must speak
      with my mother.

Your mother will wait.
I will not.
You'll speak with me now
or I will not be there
the next time you decide
you need my company,
my stories, or my touch.

11.

Somehow my words work
and he follows me,
ignores the protestations
of his bewildered friend.

I turn on him
the moment I feel
the shelter of our tree.

What is wrong with you?

     My father—

I know your father's dead.
I've held your pain
as though it were my own
though you've never once
asked about my pain.
I've given myself to you
body, mind, and soul
all the while knowing
you can never make me your wife.
And this is how I'm repaid?
Humiliated, used, disposed?

     You don't understand.

Then explain.

And so he does.

12.

One night in grief
Hamlet wandered, insomniac,
along the parapet, almost
able to imagine his father
was still upon the throne.

But then a vision, undeniable,
his father was there.
He wasn't dreaming, Hamlet insisted.
There were guards who witnessed
this apparition, who wept to tell the tale.

His father's purpose was clear:
tell Hamlet his death had not been natural.
The king's own brother, Claudius, had killed him
by dropping poison in his ear, undetectable.
And then he'd married Gertrude
as they lowered her husband's corpse
into the ground.

Poison in the ear
rang a familiar echo in my own.
The players had enacted exactly that,
on Hamlet's orders, a way to watch his uncle,
see how he reacted, to verify his father-ghost's account.

His uncle had stormed out,
a thundercloud of agitation,

            a guilty man.

I have to tell my mother!

Hamlet assumes his mother does not know.
I've always liked the queen.
She is formidable, but kind.
Still, could such a thing have happened
without her consent?

You hurt me tonight.

He starts to protest.

I understand, though I don't excuse your reasons.
To make it up to me, I ask one thing:
Before confronting your mother,
can we speak to mine?

Your mother?

I trust her wisdom.
I think you just might too.

13.

At daybreak we walk
to the cottage.

I thought I'd be shy
for him to see
my childhood home,
a garden shed to his palace.

But his face lights up
before we've stepped inside.
The garden overflows with blooms,
a pair of birds sit singing on the fence.
The boy who tends our chickens
chases one down the lane.

    It's wonderful.

I know.

Inside, the whole house is
smaller than his chambers
but more full of love
than the palace could ever be.

Now that we live at the castle
most of the cottage has become
Mother's apothecary.
Bottles clutter every surface,
pots steam on the stove.

The air is fragrant from herbs
hanging in bunches at every turn.

Taller than even Father,
Hamlet has to duck
a bunch of thyme
to make his way inside.

     It's wonderful.

I know.

At the sound of our voices
Mother emerges from the back room
and takes Hamlet in her arms.
She's never been one for the propriety of court
and she is queen of this castle.

     Dear, dear boy.
     Sit. You'll have some tea.

14.

More soothing than tea,
he has Mother's undivided care.

Hamlet tells his story,
the one he told me the night before
plus more things he's seen, ways he's suffered,
doubts he has about the queen's choices.

Mother listens, hums,
nods her interest, sympathy.

When he is done
we sit in silence
while she makes more tea.
When it's set before him
she sits again and takes his hand.

> *You've suffered far too much*
> *for one young boy. And however much*
> *your mother knew, she's suffered too.*
> *I'm afraid there's suffering still to come.*
> *But you must not bear it all alone.*
> *There are matters at play here,*
> *not only personal, but political,*
> *and they should not be on your shoulders.*
> *What I propose is this: I talk to my husband*
> *and he'll help us decide how to proceed.*

I must be allowed to
speak to my mother.

      Of course you must. And you will.
      But first let's arrange things
      so you'll approach her
      from a place of truth and love
      and receive the same from her in return.
      We love you, young prince,
      and you are welcome here.

15.

We stay at the cottage that night,
Mother, Father, and I.
Even the prince
for he doesn't believe
he can hold himself back
from confronting his mother
if he should see her,
or worse, his uncle-king.

He refuses to sleep
in one of our beds, threatens
to make for the palace where anything could happen
if we don't let him curl up on a pallet
before the hearth like a servant
or loyal dog. I sit
beside him, stroking
his hair until his breathing evens out.
I pile him with blankets,
afraid he'll wake in terror,
cold and alone.

Mother and Father speak through the night.

16.

It's madness.

    It's not.

    It is. The boy is not himself,
    he raves and says such things—

        It's grief.

    Exactly. That doesn't mean
    his tales are true. Ghosts?

Mother tells Father of the poison
in the ear of the player
and the strange reaction
of the new king.
But even more than that:

        Don't you find it odd
        that she married so quickly?
        Not just a grieving woman, but a queen.
        Her Majesty is fully capable of ruling by herself.
        She felt no need to have a man beside her; I'm sure of that.

    Yes, but—

        And her husband's brother?
        Do you not find that odd? I could see it
        if she married him two years from now,

with time for grief on both their parts
and bonding as he helped her rule.
But such haste, it seems to me,
means they had bonded well before
King Hamlet died. Don't you think?

This is dangerous talk.

Which is why we discuss it here.

He pauses, a silence so heavy
I worry it might crush my sleeping prince.

All right. You're right. I do not know for sure
but I suspect that Claudius and Gertrude
have had . . . a bond for quite some time.

A bond?

Yes.

Then doesn't that make it
all the more likely
the king was murdered?
Either as a plot between the two
or else by Claudius alone,
I do not know. For the queen
might have had a bit of amusement
with some other entertaining fellow,
but not her husband's brother
unless the feelings were deep and strong.

Do you accuse the queen of murder?

Another deafening silence.

>   *I don't believe she dropped the poison*
>   *in his ear. It's possible she didn't even know.*
>   *I do believe it was done for her love.*

They go on and on.
It seems Father agrees on substance,
but to accuse the king is unthinkable—
as good as death—and to confront
the queen might be the same,
unless she truly didn't know,
and then her response
is unpredictable.

But to do nothing
is to leave Hamlet
in such a state of disarray
that Denmark's line of succession
would be wildly insecure.

Mother proposes they approach the queen together,
not with accusations but concerns
for Hamlet's state of mind, his visions.
If Mother is there, she can assess
the reactions of the queen;
their common ground as mothers
might allow Gertrude an honesty
she'd otherwise withhold.

In the morning, they are gone.

17.

Though I've shared his bed
I've never awoken beside my prince.
I didn't mean to sleep by the hearth
but there I drifted off
and in the night his arms
have wrapped around me,
keeping me warm and cushioning me
from the stone.

         I've never slept so well.

I smile at the thought
of his massive bed, feather mattress,
luxurious silks, and always-tended fire.
He'll be hungry soon and here
there is no palace cook.
I pry myself from his arms
and roll out my neck.

I'll start breakfast.

He sits up, squinting
at the light from the window,
the only sound birdsong
and some distant laughter.

         Are your parents awake?

He's angry when I tell him
where they've gone and why

until I explain that Mother's sympathy
works magic never achieved
by angry confrontations.
He understands, having witnessed her charms,
but insists we leave for the castle right away.

In the doorway, I grab his hand,
wanting one last moment here
in this place where we are not prince and subject.

I love you.

He takes the moment.
I think we both know
it will not come again.
He kisses me, sweet.

      I love you, too, my helper.

18.

When we arrive
I half expect (more than half)
that he will send me away,
fill me in later.

Instead, he keeps a firm hold
on my hand and leads me
to his mother's chambers.

There we find
both our mothers
beside the fire,
arms around each other.

Father off to the side,
staring out the window, grim.

When Gertrude sees Hamlet,
she shakes off my mother
and leaps to her feet.

> *Oh, darling. I'm sorry!*
> *I didn't want to believe—*

She breaks down in tears.
Hamlet remains stoic,
waits for her to go on.
Finally she does
without a word from him

until she's finished
telling him how

    she and her husband's brother
    had been drawn together for many years.
    He'd made comments in moments of passion
    how different things would be
    if the king were to die, disappear.
    Perhaps she'd even made such comments herself,
    she didn't mean them; she truly
    loved her husband-king.

    But the oddities of the past few months,
    the things she never could explain
    about her husband's death

    or her new husband's strange state
    as they grieved together
    and decided to marry,
    together with his reaction to the play,
    she sees it all at last.

Even with these answers before him
Hamlet seems more muddled than before.
His mother isn't guilty of the king's murder, but
neither is she blameless. She hasn't been coerced.
She's been a woman getting what she wanted
and her son has been collateral.

When she has heaved out
her story of such woe,

all the words she'd ever known
of grief and guilt and lamentation,
he finally speaks. To all of us.

      Don't follow me.

Exit the prince.

19.

I know he will not go to our tree
if he wants solace,
if he can't face me.

But I go there anyway,
wait, hoping with time
to clear his head
or need of listening ear,
he'll find me there.

He doesn't.

We sleep at the cottage
for Father doesn't trust
Gertrude won't tell Claudius;
we would not live to see the morning.

I don't retire to my bed
but stay at the hearth all night,
pretending I feel an echo of Hamlet's
arm around my waist.

In the morning, soldiers
pound on our door.

20.

This time not the prince
But a wild-eyed queen graces
our humble home.

Your Majesty.

She doesn't see my curtsy.

     He is not here?

The prince? No, Your Majesty.

She sinks, distracted,
on the nearest chair.

My mother's hands on hers
bring the queen into focus
long enough to confer
with my parents.

But all their talk
of treachery and treason,
rallying the troops to back the queen
fades into the background
as I wonder

       where is my Hamlet?

21.

Three days later
Hamlet appears in our garden,
by the light of a full moon.

He sits next to a chicken
who has not gone home to roost,
the two of them a pair of lost souls.

I've been so worried.

      I'm sorry.

Don't be.
Have you spoken
with your mother?

He strokes the chicken
who squawks but settles
beside him, accepting their bond.

      She's going to
      execute my uncle.

Yes.

      And I'll be king.

Not right away.

      But soon enough.

We sit there,
all the things unsaid between us
sinking into the soil and taking root.
We can't be together,
not that we ever could, but now—

I'm too broken.

We all are broken.

Not like I am.

Broken people can be loved.

*Yes. But I won't drag you
into a world full of nothing
but pain and deceit.
It will break me further
to lose you, but better that
than break you too.*

I'm stronger than you think.

I know. Please stay that way.

22.

The next day
as the soldiers
put the king in chains,
as the court learns
of his treachery
and Hamlet addresses the people
and assures them of Denmark's stability,
its strong leaders, its unshaken base

I climb our tree.
I am done in this castle.
Father will still advise the queen
but Mother and I will be better off
away from the court and its unforgiving stone,
away from reminders of the boy I love.

But I need to feel its branches beneath me
one more time, the leaves rustling in my hair,
listening to my secrets. I need to ask them
to listen to my boy, to take his secrets with them
when they fall, let them return to the earth
to grow more flowers, daisies, maybe.

I climb out on Hamlet's branch,
his stage for dancing while I tell
a jolly tale, a chaise to spread his lanky limbs
upon on a lazy day in summer.
I pretend he is there.
I pretend we are one.

And then I fall.

[TRAP ROOM]

(In the trap room there's a moment of suspended breath, a moment where it's still possible that after falling, Ophelia will slice through the water with the strength of her body, the force of her will, and emerge from the river a girl ready to be queen.

But that's not how this fairy tale ends. This one is more in line with dissolving into sea-foam or dancing to death in red-hot iron shoes. If you'd like to imagine Ophelia sinking gracefully beneath the water's surface, leaving behind a perfectly arranged halo of flowers, instead of the gasping and thrashing of an actual drowning, you can have that bit of ignorance.

But she still dies.)

JULIET

You still die?!

OPHELIA

We all die. Tragedies, remember?

JULIET

But this was supposed to be you taking control, driving the story.

CORDELIA

She did that.

JULIET

Barely.

OPHELIA

I did. I did things this time. I kept my father alive! And Hamlet!

JULIET

And your mother! But not yourself!?

CORDELIA

Like she said, we all die. Unless the tale you want to tell is that you're some immortal being, there's going to be an end to your story.

OPHELIA

Right. Hamlet dies too, but no one paints his corpse. They analyze his thoughts and words—so many words. So many more words than I get. They clamor to play Hamlet, and then Lear. Who also dies. Dying isn't the problem. Being remembered only for our deaths and the moments they gave to the men onstage with us—that's what I'm over.

JULIET

But it doesn't have to be like that, at fifteen! Falling from a tree and drowning.

CORDELIA

At least she didn't kill herself this time.

OPHELIA

Who says I killed myself the first time?

JULIET

Wait, what?

CORDELIA

Gertrude. Gertrude says. She has a whole big speech about it.

(Lavinia shakes her head. Vehemently.)

JULIET

Wait, you're right. She doesn't, does she? All she says is that you fell.

OPHELIA

Climbed out on a branch and fell, drowned by the weight of my clothes.

CORDELIA

Cue hundreds of years of fetishizing art of your dead, ethereal body in the water.

OPHELIA

Artists will do what they will.

JULIET

So did you?

OPHELIA

I mean, of course I did. Isn't that what we're all doing here?

(Beat.)

CORDELIA

I wouldn't call myself an artist, personally.

OPHELIA

Storytellers are artists!

JULIET

What are you two talking about?

OPHELIA

"Artists will do what they will," I said, and you said, "So, did you?"

JULIET

I meant did you take your life.

Wait, are we artists?

OPHELIA

I think so.

JULIET

You can't *think* you took your life. I'm pretty sure you'd know.

OPHELIA

I *think* we're artists.

(Juliet snaps, gets Ophelia's focus on her. Slowly, with no possibility for misunderstanding:)

JULIET

Did you kill yourself the first time?

OPHELIA

Well.
    (Beat.)
Does it matter?

CORDELIA

Either way, she was dead.

JULIET

I don't get you two.

CORDELIA

Life's messy, princess. The sooner you realize that—

JULIET

First of all, you're the only actual princess here. And second, I grew up in a place where the streets regularly ran with blood from ancient grudges. I *know* life is messy. The very first lines of my play say I'll die. It's decided before I've made my first entrance. I refuse to accept that! Just because life is messy doesn't mean we have to give up and accept some horrible, gruesome ending.

CORDELIA

But isn't the choice your whole point? You can't say "take back the narrative" and then get mad when you don't like how she tells it.

JULIET

So you choose early death too? On the grounds of life is messy?

(Cordelia shrugs; she's not on board with this whole thing, but if she were, she wouldn't rule out death. Juliet turns to Lavinia.)

JULIET

What about you? Tell me you wouldn't change whatever happened to you!

(Lavinia is on the spot, but this time she doesn't shrink back. She would change it. Of course she would. Though if she examines the thought, she has no idea how her revision would work. To change everything that happened to her would require changing her father, for one. And not only him, but all fathers. Capital-F Fathers. The whole system.

The others are staring. She's been silent so long. So, so long. Even when she trod the boards, she was silent. Silent as she was given to a man she didn't want. Silent as she was stolen away by another. Silent while raped and mutilated. And then, when she found a way to tell her story, murdered by her father to kill his own sorrow.)

OPHELIA

You can tell us, you know.

JULIET

You've heard our stories.

(They wait. Part of Lavinia wants to tell them. But these girls don't understand the cost of telling. They don't understand that sometimes you muster the courage to clench a stick in your blood-soaked mouth and scratch into the dirt the names of the men who destroyed you. And then sometimes you're killed for your efforts. But at the very least she wants to explain why she can't tell this story. She holds up her arms, slowly, so as not to startle them. This time, they don't flinch.)

OPHELIA

I'm sorry that happened to you.

(They're still waiting, still not understanding. She's not writing it in the dirt this time. Frustrated, Lavinia makes the only sound she can. A sort of strangled grunt. For the first time they realize she physically cannot tell them. She holds one of her stumps up to her mouth, pointing, and grunts again. Intentional.

Cordelia approaches her.)

CORDELIA

May I look?

(Lavinia holds Cordelia's gaze. Something passes between the two oldest girls. The two most starved of love in their time upon the boards. One girl from the Bard's earliest attempts; the other revised and refined, but still ultimately a prop. Lavinia nods, and opens her mouth, fighting back the memory of the last time her mouth was opened at another person's whim. Cordelia sees the emptiness where a tongue should be. She sees how brutally this girl before her has been silenced.

Lavinia cannot tell them her story—as it originally happened, or as she'd have it happen, if there were a way to untangle that mess of guts.

Finally Cordelia gets it, the power in taking her story back. The privilege in having a story that can be told. She's ready. She's furious. Keeping her voice level, her gaze fierce, she tells Lavinia:)

CORDELIA

This wasn't your fault.

OUT OF THE STORM

Rose Red

My aunt Beatrice and nursemaid Grace
spend far too long selecting the dress I'll wear
for the suitors' arrivals, for the day
France and Burgundy make their cases
to marry into Father's kingdom.

> *The blue brings out the color in her eyes.*

> *But rose sets off her fairest skin.*

I pull my hair back, discouraging
Grace's preference for curls and flower crowns.

They hope to marry me for land and power,
not for my sparkling charm and pretty face.

They exchange a look.
Aunt Beatrice concedes to the rose
and Grace returns the blue gown to my closet.

> *You've always been too smart for your own good.*
> *Don't act ignorant now. Men want power, yes,*
> *but a woman's charms cannot be underestimated.*

> *Do you recall when Regan was betrothed?*
> *She knew who she wanted, wore*
> *the red of Cornwall's family crest,*
> *her bosom nearly spilling out.*
> *He waxed so poetical the other suitors*
> *never stood a chance.*

I shudder to think that matters of life and death,
war and peace could be decided by my bosom.
In agreement, Grace frowns at my chest.

I would rather not marry a man
whose love is contingent
on the size of my breasts.

> *And I would rather not*
> *have boils on my bum*
> *but here we are.*

Lady Beatrice laughs, my noble aunt
an unlikely pair with my bawdy nursemaid,
but they've been dearest friends
since I was born and together
they tended me through my father's grief,
my older sisters' mourning for our mother.

Father says the marriage is political.

Beatrice cups my face in her hands.

> *It is. But you should not keep my brother's counsel*
> *in matters of the heart. In any case,*
> *both France and Burgundy are decent men.*
> *If we must give you over to another's care,*
> *you could do worse.*

They buzz around me, making preparations
and I am left to think of how too soon

I'll be the mistress of my own home.
I'll have a husband whose marriage to me
might be political but he'll have expectations,
and I, a woman (nearly), will be the one to meet them.

Missing the Joke

By the fire in the sitting room
my sisters arrange my chess pieces
into pleasing configurations
with no regard to the problem I was solving.

  The blushing bride!

Goneril raises her teacup toward me.

I do not marry today.

  But you are blushing.

They both laugh. They laugh so easily
and half the time I do not get the joke.
I drag a chair to sit beside them;
they look at me in surprise.

Goneril has the decency to stop
wreaking havoc on my chessboard.

When your suitors came,
Father made the choice, didn't he?
Did things turn out the way you wanted?

  Father thought he made the choice.

My elder sister reaches for the tray,
pours a cup for me.

But I set my eyes on Albany the moment
I stepped in the room and steered all conversation
his way, made the others look like fools.

    I took another tack.

Regan passes me my tea.

    I made myself irresistible,
    inspiring Cornwall to rise above the rest.

    Literally.

They snicker. Again I miss the joke.
But it has something to do
with the red dress and Regan's bosom.

And how did you know? How did you decide
to set your sights on those two men?

    Albany's estate is grander, plus
    I thought his temperament better suited
    to get along with Father.

I do not care about estates,
but the rest is practical advice.
I turn to Regan. She shrugs.

    Raw sexual magnetism.

I spit out my tea and they both explode with laughter.

You think I'm kidding, but I'm not.
It matters. First time I saw Cornwall
astride a horse I saw what he'd be like
between the sheets and vowed
to make him mine. It's worked out well.

Again the expectations of a bride.
I wonder if there's a way to judge
if one of my suitors would rather value
my intellect and strategy, my years of learning
at my father's side how best to lead a kingdom?
I care not how he rides a horse.

Division

Their horses stabled,
France and Burgundy have arrived
and Father gathers us all:

       daughters, sisters' husbands,
       suitors for my hand,
       plus Beatrice, and Father's dear advisor Kent.

Today is not only about my betrothal, he says,
but also his decision to divide
his kingdom and leave us to rule
while he spends the rest of his days in leisure.
Not only that, but he'll decide
the division of the kingdom
based on our declarations of love for him.

I wait for my sisters to laugh, expose the joke.
But no one does. Kent looks dismayed, my aunt appalled.
The husbands and suitors cannot mask their intrigue.

As the eldest, Goneril performs first.
Father surely sees her gushing praise as false and cunning;
she declares a love she's never demonstrated.
Regan does the same, but even more outlandish;
the lady doth cajole too much, I think.

Then he turns to me.
I cannot do it, will not play this stupid game.
I stammer out my reasons.

When Father protests, incredulous,
I just might cave except
my aunt's eye steadies me, affirming
I should not dance his dance
to earn what is my right.

Then it turns from dance to war.

Turning Tide

Aunt Beatrice is first to intervene.

> *My brother, you know the love I bear for you*
> *and I have shown that love by raising up this girl*
> *who speaks her mind with honesty. You do her wrong*
> *to treat her so, indeed to play this game at all.*

Before Father's wrath intensifies
dear Kent adds his voice of reason.
As the tide turns, my sisters do as well,
eager to show they've walked the high ground
all along. Their husbands nod support.

I do not know my legs are trembling
until I feel a kindly hand upon my shoulder—
France's voice is gentle as his touch.

> *You do him credit as a daughter.*

There is an awful moment
when I don't know how Father will respond.
But then he laughs and praises me
for principles, chides my sisters,
then ignores my aunt, which is when I know
he was deadly serious
until he realized how it looked
and then he changed his tune
to sing the winning song.

Foothold

We are apportioned lands of equal size,
the most desirable to Goneril, the eldest.
Next to Regan, then to me.

The Duke of Burgundy seems miffed
my portion isn't quite so grand.
But France remains attentive;
perhaps he only seeks a foothold here
since he already rules a kingdom of his own.

My aunt is clearly smitten with this foreign king.
She and Kent join forces, charm offensive,
involving France in witty conversations,
excluding Burgundy until it's clear my father
has a favorite that he thinks he came to on his own.

If I could choose, I'd choose no husband.
But that is not an option.

Once Burgundy has read the room and left,
we settle in to feast. France is smart and witty
but stands his ground when Albany and Cornwall
disparage the French, no doubt jealous
of their wives' eyes on the charming king.

They're only dukes.

Political

The first time we're alone together
I walk the gardens with the man
who'll be my husband
and (I cannot help myself) I blurt:

A marriage is political.

He doesn't break his stride
or answer right away.
When he does, his words
are carefully chosen.

> *I do agree, in principle.*
> *A marriage such as ours, with the weight*
> *of nations, political indeed.*

We walk along the path.
I'm not sure I've been clear.

I'm not interested in
                    love.

Again, he's quiet for a time.

> *It seems to me you showed great love*
> *for your father when he played his little game.*

Relief washes over me
that he saw my actions in this way,

but only for a moment, overtaken
by suspicion. He means
to charm me into wanting him.

I am not without a heart.
But I'm not sure I'm capable
of romantic love, of passion.
I know heirs are expected, certain
duties as your queen, but beyond that . . .

He stops and gazes at a pair
of birds that swoop across the sky.

> *There's time to figure all that out.*
> *I'll never ask you to be someone you are not.*
> *I've allied myself with your country,*
> *your mind, and not your body.*

Fantasy

A man who wants my mind
is a thing I've dreamed about
late at night, tucked under blankets
where my body is my own.

But a man who does not want my body?
Impossible. Not because my body
is so irresistible—lack of bosom, after all—
but not wanting my body means not wanting
power over me. No such man exists.

Unless he's like the huntsman who races
to the chaplain upon each return to the palace
and it's not for confession.

Or unless he's like me?

But no. That's a fantasy
I'd never entertain,
even in the darkest part
of the night.

Packing

Whatever his motivations,
my mind and body are to follow him to France
to meet his court, his people,
and bring his family back to Britain
for the marriage celebration.

Grace's tears soak my gowns
as she packs my trunk for travel.

I'll be back soon.

    Not for long.

Even Aunt Beatrice is emotional
though she'll not only accompany me
on this voyage, but likely move with me to France.
Grace would be welcome, but she has a family here
and cannot be parted from this land, even for me.

    Your sisters await you
    in your sitting room.

I'm shocked they came to say goodbye.
This isn't final. A few weeks at most
and I'll return. My sisters aren't sentimental.

    I know they haven't always been
    your dearest friends, but listen
    to their advice. They'll have wisdom
    I never can impart.

My dear aunt, never married, has all the wisdom
I care to know. But for her I brace myself
and listen to my sisters.

The Locket

Regan lounges on my chaise
as though she's passed endless nights
in girlish conversation with me there.

Goneril stands by the fire,
looking more like Father
preparing to address generals
than confidante sharing wisdom.

   Little sister. All set to sail?

I smooth my sailing dress.
I've been out on little jaunts
when it strikes Father's fancy
to be upon the sea, but I've never
been aboard a ship to voyage
from one land to another.

I'm ready.

Regan laughs.

   Doubt it.

   Hush. She'll be fine.

Goneril pulls something
from the folds of her dress
and presses it into my hand: a locket.

This was Mother's.
We know you don't remember her
but wanted you to have it.

The locket is beautiful, delicate.
A Celtic knot engraved upon a silver heart.
I pry it open; find a lock of deep brown hair.

That's Father's. Your first true love.

Goneril hushes Regan again.

Thank you. But why give me this now?
Why not wait for the wedding?

They exchange a glance.

A lot can happen in a few weeks.
We just wanted to be sure.

Regan stands, their business done,
and sweeps toward the door.
I take Goneril's hand: It's cold and limp.

You'll take care of Father?

Regan snorts as she disappears
into the hallway. Goneril nods.

Leave him to us.

Setting Sail

Perhaps it's my sisters' strange behavior
or the cool silver locket at my throat
but as I stand at the bow of the ship
and watch the Dover shoreline recede
I cannot shake the feeling that I'll never
pass this way again.

> *Is she well?*

The wind attempts to swallow France's voice
as he speaks to Beatrice.

> *You're kind to ask.*
> *She's always had*
> *a tender stomach.*

A welcome lie.
I muster a faint smile at France
and he moves on, a liveliness in his step
I hadn't seen on land. Likely he's relieved
to put my strange family behind him.

Aunt Beatrice draws near again.

> *You'll be back. But it won't be the same.*
> *If you should shed a tear or two, no one would know.*
> *The spray of the sea is something, isn't it?*

Chameleon

The French court is not only another land,
but another world. I'm grateful the king
is pulled away the moment we disembark;
no longer must I fend off his persistent attentions.

A team of maids swoop into my chambers
to unpack my trunks, chattering in rapid French,
overwhelming me with the newness of this place.
It's then I realize the chameleon king
has spoken only in impeccable English.

My aunt's French is better than my own book learning;
she translates, relieves me of the need to interact.
At dinnertime she sends word that I'm exhausted from the voyage.

The king himself arrives at my chambers,
bearing a tray of food. Does he have nothing better to do?
I withdraw and Beatrice greets him at the door.

Whatever she needs, please let me know.

Of course, Your Majesty.

*And would you give her this?
I thought it might help her
feel more at home.*

*You're very kind.
Good night.*

Good night to you both.

Squares

Perched atop a pile of bedding
that threatens to drown me
I open the king's gift
to find the king's game:
a chess set to replace
the one I left behind,
thinking it juvenile
to bring a childhood toy
to my life as a queen.

Aunt Beatrice frowns.

> *Oh, dear. I'm rubbish at that game.*

That's all right.

I focus on the squares,
precise and even,
the same here as always.

I know how to play this game alone.

Calculation

Touring the grounds the next day
I'm closer to myself
with the wind in my hair
and green all around.

After pleasantries,
the king walks quietly.

We're headed for the stables,
where he's promised another gift.
I battle between excitement
and wariness. I breathe easier at the thought
of a horse of my own, but I also know
gifts do not come without their price.

He leads me to the stall of a beautiful stallion,
gleaming chestnut flank, distinguished mane.
This horse is clearly royalty.

> *I thought you might like him;*
> *he reminds me of the horse*
> *you rode back home.*

The resemblance is strong,
the thoughtfulness striking.
Or was it calculation?
But there is something cold in this creature's eyes.
My own eye wanders the stable.

> Of course, if you see another
> that strikes your fancy,
> you're welcome to your pick.

Truly?

> Truly. I'd give you my own steed
> if it makes you happy. I only want
> you to feel at home.

Calculation, then.

Possibility

Whatever France's reasons
for gifting me a horse,
I do not stop talking
about the slight, night-black mare
all through the day, and when dinner comes,
I allow my aunt to dress me for dinner.

There I meet the nobles of his court.
I expect to listen quietly, but the king
engages me in conversation,
laughs loudly at my stories, and his people
follow suit. They give suggestions
for what I ought to name my horse.

If the gift was a calculation
to open me up, it worked.
But I'm savvy enough
to keep both the gift and my guard.

I'm introduced to his military brass.
The captain is patronizing at first, but France
insists I'll be the queen in more than name.

> *You should see her play chess.*
> *I can't imagine how formidable she'd be*
> *with troops of flesh and blood.*

It's just one night and I am still
a stranger in a foreign land

with a man who must want things I cannot give
but with my aunt at my side
and a horse of my own,
there is possibility here.

Working Order

The weeks fly by until we're packing trunks again,
another voyage ahead of us and then,
a wedding. Alone in bed at night
anxiety blankets me. France might
welcome talk of strategy, give me
the pick of his stables,
but he is still a man.

The ladies of the court
endlessly express their envy,
what beautiful babies we'll make.
They say these things assuming my delight,
not knowing how they make me shrivel up inside.
Could a baby even grow there?

But I know it could. My aunt and nurse
have both made sure I understand
my parts and what they require,
ever since my first blood came.

I was horrified, old enough to realize
how different life would be as a boy,
but now to add this monthly insult seemed
too much to bear. When I said as much
to my sisters, they laughed.

I'm bleeding now, as I fasten
the latch on my trunk and nod
for the footman to carry it off.
It seems my parts are in working order.

Evicted

The voyage back to Dover passes quickly.
Instead of sailing into the unknown, I return
preoccupied with what it will mean to be a wife,
and how Father will receive me
but at least my aunt is constant
and Grace will greet me
at the only home I've ever known.

Everything changes
the moment we pull into port,
greeted by urgent messages from Kent.
In our absence, my sisters and their husbands
have turned upon each other
in attempts to control the land bequeathed to me.

They would have preferred I be banished.

France orders the ship to return, take back
unessential travelers who came expecting revelry
and deliver all available troops.
If this should come to war, we'll have to pick a side.

We will not take the plodding carriages that await us.
Together France and I mount the messenger's horse
and gallop full speed toward my father, the king.

Unable to gain Father's allegiance to her side,
Goneril has evicted him from the castle, his castle,
as she is now mistress of the lands it sits upon.

Regan tried to sway him to her side in the dispute
but no doubt he recalled how little love she truly bore him
when asked to account for it, and he refused.

Which leaves him stranded, wondering
when his daughters will turn so fully against him
that they do away with him completely.

But he does not know that I have come.

Peace

My sisters
could not even wait
until my wedding celebration passed
to squabble over lands
I do not even need or want.

I love Britannia, yes,
but I would give it up
to broker peace.
I've all of France now, anyway.

They did not even ask,
just barreled into war.

But Father, abdicated though he has,
would never go so easily.

Retinue

Father hunkers at a rarely used hunting cottage
with the Earl of Gloucester, wounded;
Gloucester's son Edgar, a soft-spoken, sharp-thinking young man;
and faithful Kent.

That is the king's entire retinue.
One aged advisor and two nobles with limited power.
But now he has a daughter, and the king she is—

[TRAP ROOM]

(In the trap room, Juliet interrupts.)

JULIET
Wait, who's the Earl of Gloucester?

OPHELIA
And Edgar? Have we met him?

JULIET
I don't think you need them.

CORDELIA
They were there.

JULIET
So were Romeo's parents, but I didn't mention them.

CORDELIA
But Gloucester's story is important. It's this parallel father-son thing—

JULIET
It doesn't matter.

CORDELIA
Excuse me?

JULIET
I know, I know. It's your story. But that's my point. Stick to *your* story. We don't need all these extra men.

(Pause.)

CORDELIA
Gloucester shows how vicious my sisters were.

OPHELIA

They did gouge out his eyes.

(*Lavinia recoils at this. She's lost too much already, but she still has her eyes. She glances to the corners where Cordelia's sisters stand, and then edges as far from them as she can get.*)

CORDELIA (*noticing Lavinia*)

They won't hurt you. You don't have anything they want.

(*Beat.*)

JULIET

If it's about your sisters, make it about your sisters.

CORDELIA

It creeps me out that they're here. Listening.

OPHELIA

I don't think they are. Listening.

CORDELIA

It's not even what I might say about them. More what I say about our father.

JULIET

You think they'd disagree with your portrayal of him?

CORDELIA

Not that they'd defend him. Just. They had their own experiences of him.

JULIET

I always thought it would be nice to have a sibling, to be able to commiserate about our parents. To have that one other person who completely understands the unique experience of growing up in your house.

OPHELIA

It's not always like that.

JULIET

Oh yeah, you have a brother. You don't talk about him much.

OPHELIA

There's not much to say.

CORDELIA

Can we get back to my story?

OPHELIA

Sorry.

JULIET

Aye-aye, Captain.

CORDELIA

I'll try it your way.

JULIET

I mean, you don't have to.

CORDELIA

I'm not saying you're right.

JULIET

Obviously.

CORDELIA

Just, as a thought exercise.

JULIET

Got it.

(Pause.)

OPHELIA

Well?

Retinue, revised

Father hunkers
at a rarely used hunting cottage
with faithful Kent.

That is the king's entire retinue:
one aged advisor.
But now he has a daughter,
and the king she will marry.

Kent—always steady, moderating, mild—
is in a state I've never seen before.
His hair, what's left of it, stands out
as though he's tried to yank it from his head.

But Father is worse.
He's aged a decade, maybe more.
And when he sees me throws himself at me,
desperate arms around me won't let go.

I would topple, except for France
who stands behind and steadies me,
helps me bear the weight.

> *Cordelia! Cordelia, my favorite,*
> *the only one who ever loved me.*
> *How I did you wrong!*

He weeps. My father
weeps. And I feel nothing.

This grand display
has nothing to do with love.
At least not for me. Only himself.
If my sisters should lay down arms
and let him live out his days
the way he wanted, he'd never
rend his garments and repent
of the harm he's done me.

Implicit

I sit at his feet by the fire
while Kent explains the status quo.

Both sisters have evicted the father
they claimed to love with all their hearts.
Goneril's control of the castle is absolute,
Regan rules her massive estate.
At question now is control of my lands,
which my sisters tussle over as though I've died
and not sailed across a sea.

    Cordelia's lands are Cordelia's.

France is firm.
Implicit, of course,
is that they are also his.

    The fact we'd gone away changes nothing.
    What sort of people are these?

I have no answer for that.

We sent for France's soldiers right away—

    Our soldiers.

—and once my land has been secured, my lord,
you'll always have both welcome and respect.

Three Questions

When Father and Kent are sleeping,
exhausted by their weeks under siege,
France and I are left awake.

He calculates the time until his troops arrive.

I'm not convinced my lands are worth the risk
you take to put French troops in harm's way.

He looks at me, puzzled.

We are not married yet; you could retreat.
Return yourself, your troops to safer ground.
Forget you ever met me or my kin.

The flames dance
as he stokes the fire.

> *I'd rather have a wedding than a war*
> *but something tells me life with you*
> *is going to be worth this hurdle.*
> *Marriage might be political, but*
> *that doesn't make it meaningless.*

But what on earth do you get out of it?

He sighs, sets down the poker.
I shift, uncomfortable under
his undivided gaze.

I'll answer that, if
you answer me something first.

My wariness is not that I fear he'll dissemble.
It's that he won't. But I started this. I nod.

Why does every relationship
have to be a transaction?

Why does every kindness
need a motivation?

Why do you believe
you're not worth helping
unless you must pay a distasteful price?

A lump forms in my throat,
a prickly heat behind my eyes.
Maybe the price with this man
will be ripping down the walls
and picking through the rubble
in search of my heart.

That's three questions.

Ambassador

France does not wish to speak for me
but I know my sisters.
An olive branch is less likely
to be snapped in two if offered
by a charismatic man of authority
and not the baby sister they've resented all their lives.

He'll go with Kent, who knows the lands
and I'll wait here with Father.

I may have the biggest challenge of all.

> *This is your land, your family.*
> *The troops of France are at your command*
> *and I go now as your humble soldier.*

France is about to mount his horse
and take his leave and this is where
the grateful betrothed should
throw her arms around his neck
and send him off with kisses.

My thanks to you for all your sacrifice.

Instead, I press a kiss
to the horse's nose.

Alone

Left with my father,
the king, I realize
this may be a first.

Alone, together.
No sisters, advisors, servants.
No grandeur, trappings of our roles.
No audience.

Just girl
and her father
between four walls.

Was there a moment
when I was a baby
and my mother had died
and he held me in his arms
and wept?

Weight

The weight
presses down,
everything unsaid
and everything said

the last time
we faced off,
a declaration of war
in a declaration of love.

Realizations

I sailed across a sea
and still he followed me,
each injustice magnified
by the lens of France's decency.

> One can bear the weight
> of a kingdom without
> crushing all who cross their path.

> Loving does not make one weak.

> Another voice will not drown out the first.
> Sometimes they harmonize.

There are so many things to say
and this room is too small to contain them.
To contain us.

Legacy

He speaks first.

      I'm old, Cordelia.

I've crossed a sea,
white knight upon the waves,
and he speaks of himself.

Your legacy will not be overlooked.

He shakes his head.
Foolish girl, misunderstanding.

      They weigh on me,
      the years.
      You can't understand.

This, we agree on.

But I can understand
his isolation.

Sometimes, Father, I've felt—

      I wonder, did I do enough?
      How will I be remembered?
      Will you girls drive it all
      into the ground to rot?

You did enough.

The rest is silence.

Sparrow

He dozes
and I breathe
but even asleep
he sucks the air from the room.

I go to the window
as though I might see France
galloping back, but he is barely gone.

I spy instead a sparrow, solitary.
A plump, round thing, a downy breast,
reminding me of Grace.

Why do they hurt me?

Every time my sisters
played a cruel trick,
I'd run to Grace.
She'd hold me close
and cluck her love.

> *They're hurt themselves.*
> *Hurt things lash out.*

It didn't make sense.
I could have joined them, made a trio.
We could have been hurt together.

I stopped running to Grace
not because her logic didn't help
but because I realized
my sisters would never change.

Blade

I still tried, sometimes,
to break into their circle.
They'd shove me to the ground.

Aunt Beatrice would sit,
wipe my skinned knee.

I hate them!

She'd nod.

> *I'd understand if you did.*
> *But I don't think you do.*
> *Or else you wouldn't keep trying.*

I scowled at her.

> *I grew up with your father.*

Of course she understood.
To me, Father had always been Father,
grand, imperious, controlling all.
But once he'd been a boy, skinning knees.

I should give up on them?

She was quiet for a long time.

> *It's painful to give up on family.*
> *Our hearts fight back,*

and with good reason.
If there's a chance to mend things,
you shouldn't close a door.

I should forgive them?

Oh, forgiveness.
So powerful, a blade
that can slice away rot
so a wound doesn't fester.
But take care that instrument
isn't weaponized, twisted
into the wound, leaving only you
with the pain.

Sustenance

Darkness falls.
I rummage through provisions
Kent gathered in haste
before chasing after my father
as he wandered into the storm.

There isn't much.
I encourage Father to eat.
My stomach growls
but I wouldn't keep food down.

France won't return soon.
They must travel to Goneril's grounds
and then Regan's, the lands they squabble over
so vast they require days to traverse.

When Father dozes again,
I wrap myself in a blanket.
It smells of him
and despite everything
it comforts me.

Debriefing

I can tell before France dismounts
that my sisters snapped the olive branch
and threw it on the fire.

Beside him, Kent looks exhausted,
almost as old as Father.
I help Kent down and inside the cottage,
then hurry out to talk to France.
as he leads the horses to the stream.

I take it things were not resolved with ease?

> *No. Your sisters*
> *are something.*

I snort; his eyebrow quirks.

> *Goneril's confident in her position,*
> *control of the castle, the port, and your lands,*
> *which you don't need now that you have mine.*

> *Her words.*

And what of Regan? Are her lands in play?

> *She'll leave Regan to her lands,*
> *but if Regan moves on yours, there will be war.*

I cannot comprehend my sister's mind.
She'd cast aside her family for some land?

> *It's not about the land.*

Ulterior Motives

After Goneril, France pressed on
to Regan's, where he began to understand
this feud between the sisters
once thick as blood
did not come down to land,
but a man—

[TRAP ROOM]

JULIET

Typical.

CORDELIA

What?

JULIET

Why does it have to be about a man?

CORDELIA

Your entire story is about a man! Or boy, anyway.

JULIET

Exactly. It's my entire story. Yours has enough going on without throwing in some love triangle!

CORDELIA

You didn't even let me explain it!

JULIET (*to the others*)

Is anyone else interested?

(No one is.)

CORDELIA

But it says a lot about my sisters! Goneril cheats on her husband with Edmund of Gloucester, and then Regan steals him away with her own husband barely cold in his grave!

OPHELIA

Wait, he died?

JULIET

Don't care.

Again: If it's about the sisters, make it about the sisters. I don't need the
dude.

CORDELIA

Well, dude or not, the main thing is no one's budging and there's going
to be war.

JULIET

Fine. Stick to that then.

Also you're doing it again.

CORDELIA

Doing what?

> (Juliet gives Lavinia a pointed look and Lavinia taps out the iambic
> pentameter rhythm. She knows it well.)

CORDELIA

I am not.

JULIET

Are too.

OPHELIA

You are. Just when you're speaking. I bet it's comforting.

CORDELIA

I don't need—

Will you just let me get on with it?

Courage

I stroke the horses' manes.

Are you completely disgusted by my family?

> *You mustn't think my own is any better.*
> *You simply haven't known them long enough.*
> *I'm disgusted by humanity, I suppose.*

> *But also I see you here, fighting*
> *for the father who banished you.*
> *I see Albany, faithful to his wife despite her failures.*
> *Kent, loyal to your father till the end.*

The inevitable end.

> *It looks that way.*

A battle against my own sisters.
Over what? Land, lust?
A father's favor?

What if France and I retreated,
sailed off for a kingdom
where I'd be attended as queen?

My sisters would be left
to tear each other apart,
Father caught between them.

And like France said,
there'd be battles in the French court,
just of a different kind.

> However long we have together, I'm grateful.
> I never dreamed I'd find a partner
> who speaks her truth no matter the cost.
> Who challenges me, and herself, with such courage.

My heart thunders in my chest.
I watch his lips move and still
have no desire to press my own to his
but I am starting to think I would defend this man
with my life, and maybe that's enough.

Release

What Kent told Father
while we saw to the horses
has him raging when we enter.

The words wash over me.
I've heard him rant before.
This time, stripped of everything,
I understand his indignation, pain.

But real as it is, I also know
that pain will never prompt compassion.
He'll never regret the wounds he's caused.
He'll never try to understand
why my sisters lash out,
raise armies to right the wrongs
he'll never remedy himself.

I'm not giving up on him.
I'm releasing myself from the disappointment
of expecting better, over and over again.

Favorite

Kent and France
collapse in sleep,
done in by their journey.

I thrum with nervous energy.
As soon as French troops arrive,
we'll advance on my own family.

> *You always were my favorite, Cordelia.*

I startle to realize
Father is awake.
He stares into the fire.

I was the one
who challenged you least.

> *Until you challenged me indeed.*

Well, yes. There is that.

I did not mean that as a challenge.
Only truth.
I do love you.

He is silent.

I'm not sure what that means to you.
But I know what it means to me
and I have always loved you.

Your love for me has brought you here
to the eve of a battle, of bloodshed.
What a disappointment love is.

Love

What a disappointment.
What a revelation.
What an endless breaking open
of the thing inside that fights
with every scrap of life
to stay bound up tight.

What a frightful thing, a lullaby.
What a razor-thin foundation.
What a terrifying dream,
a deluge, whisper.

A gaping wound that never heals,
pried open, vulnerable, skin peeled back.

A shelter, a pedestal,
a gift, a curse.

What a painful healing.

[TRAP ROOM]

(In the trap room, there's a long pause as the girls wait for Cordelia to go on, to tell the outcome of the battle. This is, after all, her version of the story. It doesn't have to turn out like it does most nights, with her limp body in Lear's arms. But she has told all the tale she is going to tell.)

JULIET

Wait, that's it?

CORDELIA

That's it.

JULIET

But what about the battle?

CORDELIA

What about it?

JULIET

How does it turn out? Do you vanquish your sisters? Does your father realize your true value?

CORDELIA

Life's messier than that.

JULIET

No. No! You didn't even change that much!

OPHELIA

Yes she did. She had that lovely aunt . . .

JULIET

But what happens to everyone? Who dies? Some people must die—

CORDELIA

Now you want people to die?

OPHELIA

Please say France lived. I liked him.

CORDELIA

Stories are for their readers. So, you know, you can decide.

OPHELIA

Then France lived.

JULIET

That's seriously how you're ending it? We each get to pick our own ending? Fine. You go back to France and have a happy, peaceful reign as queen, with a husband you love beside you. Bring your father with you. Forgive each other.

CORDELIA

If you say so.

OPHELIA

What about her sisters?

JULIET

Oh, forget them. Not everyone needs to be redeemed.

CORDELIA

Exactly.

(Silence.)

OPHELIA

Well?

JULIET

Well what?

OPHELIA

Now it's your turn.

JULIET

I cannot believe you.

CORDELIA

You've had an awful lot to say about our stories. I can't wait to have a go at yours.

(Beat.)

JULIET

Okay, but I was just being an engaged listener.

CORDELIA

Uh-huh. I'll be sure to engage right back. Show us how it's done.

JULIET

Fine. I will.

JULIET & ROMEO

I stumble
through the day
in a dream,
a covert bride.

Nobody knows
save Nurse and the friar
and while I cannot believe
that everyone cannot see
how I have changed
doesn't know the world
is off its axis.
I also do not mind
keeping our love
a private thing awhile longer,
a secret jewel in my heart.

I cannot comprehend
why Nurse comes to me
with such grief upon her face.

What now, dear Nurse!
Nothing can bring me down today!

> *Oh, child. I fear a brawl.*
> *Just outside the gates*
> *I passed a group of boys,*
> *both Montagues and Capulets,*
> *about to draw their swords.*

Not Romeo?

Not Romeo. Your cousin Tybalt, though—

I race for the door.
This would not be the first
brawl on our doorstep.
I've never felt the need to intervene
but now I feel it keenly:
                            the absurdity, the waste.
Romeo has not a violent bone in his body
but in the right circumstances, to defend a friend,
to defend his love for me, he just might draw his sword.

Not Romeo but Tybalt,
my darling almost-brother cousin,
blade drawn, face aflame with rage.

He squares off with a Montague.
Romeo's friend, I think,
though I'm not sure
for at the ball
they all wore masks.

It matters not if he is dear to Romeo.
Either way this bloodshed serves no purpose;
it only builds more walls.

Tybalt, no!

All action halts as I throw myself
before my cousin's sword.

> *Are you mad, cousin?*

Are you? What can possess you
to draw your weapons in the streets?
What possible reason do you have
to invite bloodshed here?

> *These filthy Montagues made mockery*
> *of your father's ball, our family name,*
> *dared show their faces in your very home.*

Indeed I don't believe they did
for all were masked that night.

Someone snickers.
I hope it was a Capulet
for Tybalt has spilt blood for less.

Cousin, go back inside.
This doesn't concern you.

How on earth does this not concern me?
Am I not a Capulet? Is my life not governed
by this ridiculous feud? Can you even tell me
what it's all about, besides a reason for you
to swing your sword and feel like a man?

I am protected by the love he bears me.
He will not harm me, though
the look in his eyes causes doubt.
If I don't tread lightly, these Montagues
might pay the price for his wounded pride
as soon as I have turned my back.

His eyes jerk away from my face
as I hear commotion behind me
and then the ringing of unsheathed weapons.

Get away from her!

Romeo is there, his blade
pointed at Tybalt's heart.

Romeo, no! Don't!
He is my cousin!

Romeo's eyes flicker to me;
he does not drop his sword.

> *He threatens you.*

> *Say another word to her*
> *and I will run you through*
> *like the dog you are.*

Enough! Enough, the both of you.
All you foolish boys with nothing more to do
than play at war. Too privileged to end up
on an actual battlefield, still you insist
on pointless feuds to make you feel like men.
Can a single one of you tell me
what this grudge is about?

I survey the boys gathered around me.
That's what they are—boys.
Romeo and Tybalt, both dear to my heart.
Romeo's friends, and a few more of my kinsmen,
ready to spill blood on Tybalt's order.
Finally Tybalt speaks, his voice full of bluster
but his words empty.

> *Montagues are dogs.*

Why? What makes them so?

> *Their very name.*

They'd say the same of you, of me.
Are we defined by Capulet?

Are you passionate, courageous,
quick-witted, and strong because
a string of letters makes you so?

Can you truly say
this doesn't concern me
when your foolish feuds
stand between me
and the man I love?

Shock, revulsion roll over Tybalt's face.

> *You're a child.*
> *You can't know—*

I am the same age as my mother
when she was wed to Father.

> *It wasn't her choice.*

Exactly. Don't you want
better for me?

> *Not a Montague.*

Not a Montague, an abstract
target for your hate. Romeo,
who sees beyond my name.

Tybalt, I pray you. If you ever loved me,
sheathe your weapon and swear
you will not wield it again
in the name of my honor.

The next few moments stretch out
longer than the generations of this feud.
The most likely outcome
is Tybalt calls for guards to pull me inside
and then spills all the Montague blood
he can manage. Instead his sword lowers.

Thank you, cousin.

      Hear this, cousin.

He spits the word at me
as though it's as vile
as Montague in his mouth.

      *Your father may have let them
      run rampant through his ball
      but he will not waste his daughter's
      purity on a Montague.*

I silently implore my love
to master his temper.

I'll deal with my father.

      *Do it by the morning
      or I will do it for you.*

[TRAP ROOM]

(In the trap room, Cordelia interrupts with perhaps more glee than is warranted.)

CORDELIA

Okay, no.

JULIET

What are you doing? I'm not finished!

CORDELIA

This is absurd. You're just going to tell them to stop the feud and they stop?

OPHELIA

Just this one fight. Not the whole feud.

JULIET

Thank you.

CORDELIA

So you ask nicely, and Mercutio doesn't die?

OPHELIA

Neither does Tybalt. And Romeo doesn't get banished. It's a much better story.

JULIET

Again, thank you.

CORDELIA

If we're talking strictly from a storytelling perspective, it's not actually a better—

JULIET

I'm not trying to be the Bard! I'm trying to make my own choices for a different outcome.

CORDELIA

You had plenty to say about my choices.

JULIET

But I let you make them.

CORDELIA

"If it's about the sisters, make it about the sisters. I don't need the dude."

(Pause.)

JULIET

Fine. I'm sorry about that. Can I proceed now?

CORDELIA

Be my guest.

All through dinner
I struggle to find the words
to tell my father I've married Romeo.

Tybalt never issues empty threats
and if I am not the one to break this news—
that way madness lies.

But if I play it right
there could be peace.
I still believe this.

Right after I came in from the street
I sent Nurse with word for Friar Laurence
to come and help me but so far

I am on my own.

Father.

     Yes, my love.

I've been thinking.

     A dangerous pastime.

He chuckles.

Mother was my age
when you were wed.

Mother's head snaps up
from where she's drowning
herself in wine.

>*Indeed she was.*
>*Such a beauty.*

I never thought
I'd feel ready so young
but—

>>*You're not.*

Mother clenches a handkerchief
in a white-knuckled fist.

>*Let her speak.*

It's just lately I feel
like perhaps there could be
a purpose to my betrothal.
That it could do something important.

>>*You don't know what you're saying.*

>*I think she's very clever.*

>>*Juliet—*

>*Bianca, enough.*
>*See to the final course.*

I cringe as Mother is sent away.
I didn't mean for that to happen
and cannot tell Father without her here.
She glares at me and stalks to the kitchens,
her handkerchief still mangled in her hand.

That's all, Father.
But now I'm very tired.

      Yes, yes, darling.
      Let's speak more of this
      in the morning, shall we?

We shall
or else
my cousin
will beat me
to it.

Though she gripped it
like a raft on the seas,
Mother will release
her used-up handkerchief
at the earliest opportunity.

After all, a handkerchief
must be white.

No stain permitted
upon this thing
meant for wiping tears
and sweat, grime and life.

It's not that she discards
every used-up hankie.

      (That would be impractical
        —though a used-up girl . . .)

It's just that the maids must work
domestic magic to transform it
into something Mother can pretend
has never served its purpose.

[TRAP ROOM]

(In the trap room, the youngish woman stirs, the one who helped Lavinia when she first crashed through. She knows of handkerchiefs too well. Handkerchiefs given as gifts of love, dyed with the blood of virgins, used against her as proof of her impurity, as justification to smother her in her bed. She would tell Juliet, if she could rouse herself from her corner, not to judge her mother too harshly. That soiled handkerchiefs have brought down more than one unsuspecting woman.)

CORDELIA

Hold up.

JULIET

What?

CORDELIA

I'm just trying to understand.

(Beat.)

JULIET

Understand what?

CORDELIA

You're comparing yourself to a used handkerchief.

JULIET

So?

CORDELIA

Do you not see how messed up that is?

OPHELIA

It's a metaphor.

CORDELIA

Yes, thank you.

JULIET

For purity.

CORDELIA

I know. And if you have sexytimes, you're . . . snot-covered?

OPHELIA

Or something like snot.
  (Everyone looks to Ophelia in surprise.)
What?

CORDELIA

So if sex makes you impure, does that make your mother impure?

JULIET

No, because she's only had sex within the confines of marriage.

CORDELIA

As far as you know.

So according to the church, if your father gives you to Paris as a business transaction, that loveless sex is pure. But if you and Romeo get busy out of actual, mutual desire, that's a blight on your record?

JULIET

I thought you didn't care about desire.

CORDELIA

It's complicated. But it seems wrong that people who do should have to suppress it.

OPHELIA

So we should all just act on our impulses?

CORDELIA

Definitely not.

But the ones that don't harm anyone else? I'm thinking yes.

> (Pause. Cordelia's words ripple out through the trap room. The girls
> around her are young; they agree. The older women have had more time to
> be infected—stained, if you will—by all they've been taught. But if they
> keep listening, they'll learn some things from these young ones.)

I've made a mess of things.

I unburden myself to Nurse
while she brushes my hair
and readies me to sleep,
        not that I will tonight.

        You're growing. You're going to need new gowns.

I frown at her in the glass.
She is easily distracted but
usually tries to listen.

Did you hear me?
Everything is such a mess.

        Yes. I'm going to need to sort through
        all your things, make room in your closets.

Nurse—

        Listen to me, child, for you are smart, not wise.
        When I must undertake a task like cleaning your closets,
        I remove everything, not just the gowns, but also gloves
        and petticoats and underthings. I spread them out
        to see what stays, what goes, what must be mended.
        The mess gets so much worse I consider
        laying myself to rest among your silks.
        But when I stay with it, through the necessary mess,
        your closet is put to rights, leaving only what fits you best.

Tears spring to my eyes.

You don't think I've bungled this completely?

    Oh, you certainly have.
    But not beyond fixing, dove.

When she sends me out to my balcony
I don't dare hope Romeo will be there.
He cannot approach the house now.

I never dream he'll step out
from the shadows, not down below, out of reach,
but here on the balcony, in the flesh.

Romeo!

I throw myself at him,
nearly knocking us both
over the railing.
What a story that would be,
what hard-hearted storyteller,
cynical and cruel,
would bring together not only
two lovers but great shining
hopes for peace, only to send them
to their mutual deaths
on the stones below?

> *I couldn't be without you*
> *a moment longer.*

I haven't told my father yet.

> *I know. The friar got called away*
> *and I intercepted your nurse's message.*
> *I thought if I came, reminded you*
> *what we're fighting for—*

I haven't forgotten!
Oh, don't think that.
It's just that—

> *I understand. I do.*
> *You were so strong today*
> *in the street, among those swords.*
> *I hate that you had to be*
> *the voice of reason.*

I don't want to be the voice
of anything right now, with Romeo
before me, his lips
there for kissing.
I press mine to his
for a glorious moment
and then pull back.

Does Nurse
know you're here?

> *She does. And if I am not mistaken*
> *she will have vacated the room by now.*

I push him toward the bed;
he stumbles back, surprised.

My lips are frantic, hands
tugging as though I can pull
him close enough he'll never leave.

This time he is not
a boy I've danced with
boy I've kissed, but man
I call my husband.

I don't need
the blessing of the church
to know I need this boy,
I need this man beside me.

We fall onto the bed,
a mess of limbs, teeth crashing
sobs and laughter intermingled.

I want you.

I push him
onto his back.

I want
everything.

He is sweet and slow but
something desperate unfurls inside me.

I need his skin on mine
I need his lips everywhere
I need his hands to hold me together
or I might split into a thousand pieces

his skin is hot; I dive into the flame
his lips, his tongue, his hands traverse lands
I've never explored and never want to leave

I'm shattered and whole and his

and mine

[TRAP ROOM]

CORDELIA

I'm sorry, hang on.

JULIET

Oh my god, what now?!

OPHELIA

She just got to the good part!

CORDELIA

Says you.

That's the same story you told before.

JULIET

It is not. The dinner—

CORDELIA

The bedroom. What happened in the bed.

JULIET

Oh. Yeah. I mean . . . some stories don't need changing.

Now will you shut up and let me tell my story?

(Lavinia laughs. They all turn to her in surprise. Even she is surprised, realizing for the first time that she can still laugh. The others join her as Juliet continues.)

Our limbs are still entangled
as morning light breaks through
the haze of love-drunk sleep,
but more alarming the entrance
of my nurse who yanks the covers
off us with no warning.

Nurse!

      Don't Nurse me! Your father comes.

Romeo leaps from the bed
without a stitch to cover his form,
which I wouldn't mind except for
the circumstances. Which include Nurse
not even trying to avert her eyes.

      Don't look at me like that. He's not
      got anything I haven't seen before.
      Get up and dressed and try not to look
      as though you've spent the night in ecstasy.

She grabs his clothes
from where they fell
and shoves them at him.

      Out! To the balcony and get you gone.
      And you, young miss, no time for dress
      but run this brush through that mess on your head.

I follow her orders
for my brain is still stuck

in the night before, the early morning,
the haze of love
and I am ill-prepared
for a visit from my father
in the earliest hours.

Ah, good, you're awake.

As Father bursts through the door,
Nurse kicks a stray shoe of Romeo's
beneath my bed.

Father. Is something wrong?

> *Wrong? No! Things are
> exactly as they should be.*

Mother follows and that's when I sit up,
concern breaking through my haze;
at this hour she should be kneeling in the chapel .

> *Perhaps we could let her dress
> and speak of this at breakfast?*

I catch a glimpse of movement
out on the balcony
from the corner of my eye
and pray no one sees my love
as he climbs (with one shoe) to the ground.

> *Nonsense, she's awake!
> And breakfast shall be for celebrating
> with Count Paris. My girl,
> you must dress for your betrothal;
> that's what we celebrate.*

I'm past betrothal; I am wed
and my brain can't process
his words. Nurse sees my confusion.

So sorry, Master Capulet,
my old brain cannot keep up.
For what occasion shall I dress our girl?

For her betrothal to Count Paris.
After what you said last night, my dear,
I sent word to this auspicious man
who many times has expressed
his interest in your hand
and told him you were ready!
He'll be here shortly to celebrate!

My heart stops. My heart that just an hour before
beat in time with Romeo's, my husband's.

Father, no! I cannot!

He looks at me as though I've spoken French.
Then turns to my nurse.

How about that sunshine-yellow dress?
I always liked that one.

No, Father, you don't understand—

Mother crosses to me,
takes the hairbrush from my clenched hands
and starts to brush my hair herself. I can't recall
if she has ever done this task.

It's normal to be nervous, dear.
But you spoke your heart last night

and Father listened. You're a lucky girl.
Paris is a good man, kind.
You'll be lady of a grand estate
and soon you'll have children of your own—

I'm already wed!

They think I'm mad, spouting
nonsense out of fear.

They cannot fathom the idea
that I might have made my own choice
taken my own action.

They think me old enough to wed
if they have chosen it, but not
if I'm the one to fall in love.

Nurse tries to interject, support me
but I stop her. I do not want her
blamed for what she knew.

When they will not listen
to reason, explanations,
I stand my ground, repeat
my truth.

I am already married.
I made the choice to love
a Montague named Romeo.

I am already married.
I made the choice to love
a Montague named Romeo.

I am already married.
I made the choice to love
a Montague named Romeo.

You must stop this nonsense!
Paris will be here any moment!

Then I will tell him
what I have told you,
for it is the truth.

While Father rages, Mother sits quietly
at my vanity. I long to grab the rosary
from her worried fingers and shout
at her to listen, but then I see
she does not pray but stares into the glass
perhaps imagining herself in my place,
a choice between my father
and a forbidden love.
Perhaps there was such a love
and she does not imagine, but remembers.

I don't understand why you would sit there
at dinner last night and make a fool of me!

I sat there, trying to figure out
how to tell you this very truth.

I am already married.
I made the choice to love
a Montague named Romeo.

A servant knocks,
petrified to interrupt
but urged on by my nurse.

>*Excuse me, Signor Capulet,*
>*but visitors have arrived.*

Father tugs at what little hair he has.

>*Paris has come! You won't say a word.*
>*We'll get this supposed marriage annulled*
>*and he never needs to know—*

>*Pardon me, Signor. The visitors*
>*are Friar Laurence, and a young Montague.*

Father is speechless. Mother stands.

>*Tell them we'll be there shortly.*

She steers Father toward the door
and over her shoulder she says,

>*Get dressed. Something joyful.*

I've never dressed so quickly.
I don't know if the marriage
can be annulled without my consent
but it's not beyond Father to try.

It's also not beyond any member
of this household to draw a sword
on Romeo, though I have to hope
the friar's presence will dissuade
impulsive violence.

Mother is the piece of the puzzle
I didn't expect. But then she's always
been an entire puzzle unto herself.

I wear the sunshine yellow.
Not to spite Father, truly,
but because it is joyous
and despite everything
I still feel joyful.

Mother engages Friar Laurence
while Father paces, glaring at my love,
who stands watchful behind the friar's chair.

His face lights up when I walk in
and mine flushes with the memory
of his skin on mine an hour earlier.

Ah, good, Juliet has joined us!

The friar stands, embraces me,
and bids me sit beside him.

*These young people
are full of fire, are they not?*

Mother laughs; Father doesn't.

*I must confess, Signor Capulet,
that I deserve a generous portion
of your ire, for not only did I wed
these two, but I encouraged the union.*

If it were not for the presence of servants
who could spread the word around Verona
I believe Father might strike a holy man.

He remains silent as Friar Laurence
explains his position, his belief in our love,
that not only does Romeo bring equal wealth
to a match as Count Paris, but that our union
might heal what is rotten in Verona.

You speak as though you understand
these things, Friar. You do not.
Two foolish children cannot erase
these years of enmity.

What can then?

All heads turn toward Mother.
If not for the presence of the friar,
I am certain Father would strike her.
She stands her ground and continues.

Do you believe this feud must last forever?
Blood must eternally spill, loves must always
be forbidden, anger must fester in the hearts
of generations upon generations?
Is that what you want?

Of course it's not what I want, woman.
It simply is what is.

It doesn't have to be.

I go to stand by Romeo,
take him by the hand
trust his love to hold me up.
If Mother can stand her ground
with Father, so can I.

It takes so much more courage
to lay down arms than

go into battle. I will fight
for this love, but I will not
fight against you, or Montagues,
for I love both. My heart is not
for you to control, is not a pie
that can only be divided
in so many pieces, and once divided,
it's gone. It's a flower, a rose
that grows with care and sunlight,
and with enough attention, seeds will fall
and create more roses, more seeds, more love.

Father stands, staring into the fire
the whole time I've spoken, but finally
he turns. Tears line his cheeks.
He crosses the room to stand before me.
Everyone tenses, but I don't.
He brings a hand to my face.
He could strike me, but he wants
this rose to bloom.

My darling Juliet. Of Montague.

[TRAP ROOM]

OPHELIA

Okay, hang on.

JULIET

What? No! Not you too!

OPHELIA

I'm really sorry. It's lovely and romantic and I really like the rose
metaphor—

CORDELIA

You don't think it was kinda overwrought?

OPHELIA

I mean, it could use refining . . .

JULIET

What is your point?

OPHELIA

It's just so hard to believe. After all those years of bloody feuding, a
father just sets it all aside and listens to his daughter?

CORDELIA

No, no, he doesn't.

JULIET

Mine does! In *my* story!

OPHELIA

I want that to be true. I do. But even if it is, you're supposing it'll be
enough. That all the rest of the Capulets and Montagues are going to go
along with it.

JULIET

First of all, I never said that. Because you two won't let me finish! But is it so hard to believe that one girl's conviction could change the course of things? Is it so unfathomable that some men should listen, that love could change the course?

CORDELIA

Yes. And also, while we're stopped, if you're such a history-altering girl, why do you need Friar Laurence to swoop in and save you from your father?

OPHELIA

Okay, that's all her, not me.

JULIET

Friar Laurence did no such thing! I told my father myself! I told him and told him and told him. I brought Friar Laurence in because one of the choices I'm making is to give myself more support in this story. You both did that too! Ophelia got to keep her mother. You gave yourself that lovely aunt. Having support and help is not the same as letting someone else drive your story.

That's all I'm trying to do—drive my story! That was the whole point of this! And you two are being absolute monsters. Sorry, Ophelia, more her than you, but even you. Because here I am, about to come to a glorious happy ending, which is what I choose if I get to choose, and maybe it's true that I don't get to choose in the real world, that I'm more likely to end up dead at the end of a dagger or else miserably wed, and you have to interrupt me to offer your well-actuallys.

Well actually, no! Well actually, this is my story! I'm sorry you can't conceive of stories with happy endings, but I let you tell yours how you wanted to, because the choice is the point. I respected your choice. So now I choose to tell mine. To finish mine. And if you don't like it, you don't have to listen. But my story is no less meaningful if I don't die tragically.

I deserve your respect.

(Silence.)

CORDELIA

You're right.

OPHELIA

So right. I'm so sorry.

CORDELIA

I'm sorry too.

(Beat.)

So what are you waiting for? Are you going to give us this happy ending or what?

This time
no one wears masks
as we dance together,
Montagues and Capulets.

Tybalt is stormy
but my friend Rosaline
drags him onto the dance floor
and I think her charms
just might make him forget
the hate he's learned.

Count Paris is there,
dancing with Romeo's cousin,
happier than anyone ever dreamed.
Peace in Verona will be good
for his business and many girls
clamor to be his wife.

Nurse looks the gloomiest;
perhaps her life will change most of all.
But just because I'm wed
doesn't mean I won't need
her warmth and wisdom, love.

I pull her to the dance floor
and swing her in a circle.
When we're both dizzy
we lean on each other
and sway, forever entwined.

I was never a substitute for Susan.
I was a second chance for Nurse
to love, to share her heart.
And she, for me, was home.

Mother
takes me in her arms
for a spin around the floor,
a thing she's never done
but somehow feels right.

The tempo slows
and rather than push me away
she draws me close.

> *I want you to know, dear girl,*
> *I always saw you as a miracle.*
> *My body had tried and failed*
> *so many times to create life,*
> *I had given up.*

> *But then you came along.*
> *You would have been my miracle*
> *even if you'd had the life expected of you*
> *but you've done so much more.*
> *I'm so proud of you. You make me believe*

> *I have done something*
> *good in the world.*

Across the dance floor
I spot a girl with daisies in her hair.
I've never noticed her before.
She's not quite of this world, ethereal.

Another girl beside her looks
as though she just dismounted from a horse.
Windblown hair, determined jaw.

A third with eyes
that tell me a million stories
her lips never will.

They're disoriented, these girls,
unsure what force propelled them here
to a world not their own.

They aren't together and yet
the wispy one reaches out
and takes the others' hands.

Soon enough they can return
to their own stories.
For just one song, I bid them
join me on the floor.

We dance.

[TRAP ROOM]

(In the trap room, they dance.

Only Juliet, at first. All beating heart and pulsing need, she's always been made of movement. She left the stage before she'd had a chance to disconnect completely from her body, her rhythm. Remembering a ball a million years ago—or yesterday—she offers a holy palmers' kiss to Ophelia.

Ophelia takes the offered hand, lets herself be pulled up out of the muck, out of the waters that would weigh her down if she let them. Once she told stories to a dancing boy; now it's her turn, dancing not on a branch but through this maze of corners, this place that felt so much like a trap, an inevitability, but has turned out to be something else entirely.

Juliet plucks a bedraggled flower from Ophelia's hair and tucks it behind her own ear. She doesn't know its name or what it represents; she only knows it calls to her, and that's enough. She twirls Ophelia in a giddy circle until they're out of both balance and breath, but they hold one another up.

Cordelia is not a dancer, but she can keep a beat.

It's not until she sees Lavinia begin to move, though, that Cordelia shakes out her shoulders, remembers she has hips. For Lavinia has not told them her story. Even with a tongue and hands, it might be too difficult. Not all stories can be told. Some are so dark and twisted, their telling would undo the world.

But just because she doesn't speak doesn't mean Lavinia can't share who she is, what she's been through, who she'll be, if given the chance. It's in the shake of her head, defying those who would silence her. The arms flung wide to take up the space denied her up above.

Cordelia sees a magic in Lavinia that she's never seen in another person before. She cannot take Lavinia's hand, but places a gentle hand on her elbow. The girl startles out of the depth of her dance to see this girl who has so intimidated her. Cordelia is still stiff—more marching soldier than dancing girl—but she's there. She's trying.

Lavinia nods her consent for Cordelia's touch, and sways into it. Cordelia responds in her way, and they move together. Telling each other their stories.

From their corners, the older women look on, some amused, some disdainful. Some warring with the constraints still upon them. How many times have they crashed through the boards to end up here, to await their turn to repeat the cycle? Has it ever occurred to them to reach out, to share their stories, to dance? Why not?

What do these young ones have that they do not? Is it too late for them?

Some turn away, afraid of the answer. Some search the dusty corners of their minds to remember what it felt like to be free, if they ever were. A few dare to hope they'll feel it again.

Juliet and Ophelia have regained their balance, taking each other in their arms and waltzing grand circles around Cordelia and Lavinia. Proper court decorum, mingled with goofy faces and bursts of laughter. All they've learned, on their own terms.

The older girls still, open up their circle, and the younger ones rush into the void that must be filled. They lean on one another, heads on shoulders, arms on waists, hearts in hands.

The girls won't dance forever. That would be fairy-tale torture.

But for now they've been unburdened. Their hearts are light. And they're not alone.

They dance.)

AUTHOR'S NOTE

I love Shakespeare. I named my daughter for one of his characters. I have a tattoo of a quote from *Much Ado About Nothing*. I have an entire garden devoted to plants mentioned in his plays. I think he had an extraordinary gift for taking familiar stories and transforming them into works of art that would resonate with not only the audiences of his day, but for decades and centuries to come. And obviously an astonishing gift for language.

I also know an overreliance on his work has crowded out more diverse voices. He was far from infallible. There is much to criticize in his plays. I believe we can love things and also examine where they fall short. That's what I've tried to do in *Enter the Body*. One of the things I admire most about Shakespeare is how he took established stories and made them his own, highlighting what he thought was most important, ruthlessly excising what didn't suit the story he wanted to tell, and inventing what he felt was missing. I like to think he'd approve of what I've done here.

TIMELINE

The dates surrounding Shakespeare's life and the writing of his plays are approximate, to say the least. Scholars have spent a shocking amount of time on it, honestly. For me, the actual dates matter less than the big picture—exploding onto the London theater scene in his mid-twenties and working steadily for around twenty-five years (not only as playwright, but performer, director, and producer as well). And even if it's not precise, a broad understanding of the order of his plays is of interest to me—in particular how the development of his female characters changes as he matures both as a person and a writer.

The play names in bold include the characters in *Enter the Body*, both our principals and the supporting cast throughout the trap room.

APRIL 23, 1564	Shakespeare born in Stratford-upon-Avon, England.
NOVEMBER 27, 1582	Married Anne Hathaway (he was eighteen, Hathaway was twenty-six).
C.1589–1592	Shakespeare first appears on the London theater scene. In this time, he writes **Titus Andronicus (Lavinia);** *The Two Gentlemen of Verona* (probably); *The Taming of the Shrew;* **Henry VI, Part 1 (Joan of Arc);** *Henry VI, Part 2; Henry VI, Part 3;*
1595	*Edward III;*
1597	*Richard III; Richard II;* ***Romeo and Juliet* (Juliet);**
1598	*The Comedy of Errors; Love's Labour's Lost; Love's Labour's Won* (which is lost); *A Midsummer Night's Dream; King John; The Merchant of Venice; Henry IV, Part 1;*
1599	*Julius Caesar;*
1600	*Henry IV, Part 2; Much Ado About Nothing; Henry V; As You Like It;*
1602	*The Merry Wives of Windsor;* **Hamlet (Ophelia, Gertrude);** *Twelfth Night;*
1603	*Troilus and Cressida;*
1604	*Measure for Measure;* **Othello (Desdemona, Emilia);**
1605	*All's Well That Ends Well* (timing totally unclear on this one); *Timon of Athens* (maybe? who's to say);
1606	***King Lear* (Cordelia, Regan, Goneril);**
1608	***Antony and Cleopatra* (Cleopatra);** *Pericles, Prince of Tyre;*
1609	*Coriolanus* (maybe?);
1611	**Macbeth (Lady Macbeth);** *The Winter's Tale; Cymbeline; The Tempest;*
1613	*Henry VIII* (a performance of which set the Globe Theater on fire, literally).
APRIL 1616	Shakespeare dies (age fifty-six), survived by wife Anne and two daughters, Susanna and Judith.

ACKNOWLEDGMENTS

This book was one of the most joyful writing experiences I've ever had. Written during the height of the Covid-19 pandemic, we were all on constantly shifting ground. Surrounding myself with beloved characters I'd known since I was a teenager gave me something familiar to grasp onto. But also the perpetual uncertainty allowed me a unique freedom to throw conventions to the wind and truly play. Would this book even be published? Who knew? But to my great delight, it was, thanks to the efforts and support of many, including my wonderful, theater-loving agent Jim McCarthy, who said yes unreservedly when I told him I wanted to write a book that was also sort of a play. Your trust is the foundation from which I keep taking risks.

Editor Andrew Karre never knows what he is going to get when I send him a new project. But every time he dives in with enthusiasm and emerges with incredible insights that shape the work in immeasurable ways. Thank you for, among so many other things, watching *Titus* when I could not.

The team at Dutton and Penguin Young Readers does countless things behind the scenes (and beneath the stage and up on the catwalks) to make my words on the page into the book you hold in your hands. A standing ovation to Julie Strauss-Gabel, Natalie Vielkind, Melissa Faulner, Anne Heausler, Anna Booth, Rob Farren, and Jennifer Dee.

Theresa Evangelista somehow managed to create a cover that perfectly reflects this indescribable book: Thank you for doing the impossible. The school and library team—Rachel Wease, Venessa Carson, Trevor Ingerson, Carmela Iaria, and Summer Ogata—is the absolute best at working to get books into the hands of the perfect readers, teachers, and librarians. Thank you all!

Speaking of teachers and librarians—thank you all for your incredible work, and for passing my books along to young readers. Thank you to sales reps and indie booksellers as well for this work.

Thank you to Laura Shovan for feedback on the earliest draft. I kept this book pretty close, but thanks also to the following writing friends who may not have given feedback on this book, but who have provided incredible support in other ways: Jessica Lawson, Tara Dairman, Alliah Agostini Livingstone, Miriam Schiffer, Rachel Lynn Solomon, Tess Sharpe, and Rajani LaRocca.

Many thanks to Dahlia Adler, for inviting me to contribute a story to her young adult anthology of Shakespeare retellings, *That Way Madness Lies*. When I was through writing that story, I knew I wasn't done exploring the young women of Shakespeare's tragedies. That's when I began this book. *Performing Shakespeare's Women: Playing Dead* by Paige Martin Reynolds was critical in helping me articulate the gut responses I've had to many of these plays for years.

Thank you to my daughter Cordelia for the use of her name. You were named for Shakespeare's Cordelia. But the Cordelia I wrote wasn't based on you.

To my Cordelia, as well as my son Joaquin and my husband Mariño: I do love nothing in the world so well as you.

DISCUSSION GUIDE
by Sarah Mulhern Gross

1. Much of the interaction between the women in the story takes place in the trap room, a liminal space that seems to serve as a threshold between reality and the stories written by Shakespeare. Trap rooms are often used to store scenery and props, and can also be used for special effects on stage. Why do you think McCullough chose to have Shakespeare's female characters meet in this space?

2. How do Juliet, Ophelia, and Cordelia differ in their relationships with their fathers? What about Lavinia, who is unable to tell her own story in the book?

3. What role do mothers play in the stories Shakespeare created for Cordelia, Juliet, Lavinia, and Ophelia? What role do mothers or maternal figures play in the women's rewritten stories in the last part of the book?

4. Throughout the book, the reader learns more from and about Cordelia, Juliet, Lavinia, and Ophelia. However, there are other women in the trap room, too. They flutter about the edges, listening and watching in some cases, wrapped up in their own stories. We know Cordelia's sisters are on the periphery, but who else might these women be? Which female Shakespearean character would you add to the conversation?

5. How do societal expectations of femininity limit the agency and autonomy of female characters like Juliet, Ophelia, Cordelia, and Lavinia in Shakespeare's stories? What examples can you find in the book of the female characters challenging or conforming to these expectations?

6. In *We Should All Be Feminists*, Chimamanda Ngozi Adichie makes the point that the concept of gender tells us how we "should" be in society. What messages do you see in Shakespeare's stories about how women "should" behave versus how men "should" behave? How do you think those expectations affect the characters? In the last part of the story, the characters retell their stories and change them—how do they subvert patriarchal expectations?

7. On pages 164–166, Juliet asks Cordelia about her sisters and points out that the version of them Cordelia paints for the reader is one-sided. While Ophelia points out that the sisters do "gouge out a man's eyes and cheat on their husbands and kill each other, basically," Juliet pushes Cordelia to consider what might have made them that way. How do you imagine Goneril and Reagan ended up the way they did?

8. In a patriarchal society, a woman who refuses to submit to male authority is seen as a threat, and Cordelia, Juliet, Lavinia, and Ophelia are no exception. Discuss how the women's original stories, as written by Shakespeare, reflect the social and political conditions of Elizabethan times. How do their rewritten stories upend the conditions of these times?

9. Juliet repeatedly pushes back when Cordelia refers to her love for Romeo as "teenage stupidity." Cordelia sees the younger female characters as immature. Do you agree with Cordelia or Juliet? Why?

10. On page 212, Ophelia points out that:

    > Hamlet dies too, but no one paints his corpse. They analyze his thoughts and words—so many words. So many more words than I get. They clamor to play Hamlet, and then Lear. Who also dies. Dying isn't the problem. Being remembered only for our deaths and the moments they gave to the men onstage with us—that's what I'm over.

    Do you agree with Ophelia? Are the women in Shakespeare's tragedies only remembered for the "moments they gave to the men onstage" with them?

11. Lavinia is the only named character in the story who never speaks. Her tongue is cut out on stage each night, so she is unable to tell her story in the trap room, but she listens intently and the other women include her in their conversation. Why do you think the author included a silent character in the story? If you are familiar with *Titus Andronicus*, how do you think Lavinia would change her story if she could participate in the final act of the book?